BRING THE NIGHT

BRING THE NIGHT

A NATE ROSS NOVEL

J.R. SANDERS

LEVEL
BEST BOOKS

First published by Level Best Books/Historia 2023

Copyright © 2023 by J. R. Sanders

This novel is entirely a work of fiction. The names, characters and incidents portrayed in it are the work of the author's imagination. Any resemblance to actual persons, living or dead, events or localities is entirely coincidental.

J. R. Sanders asserts the moral right to be identified as the author of this work.

First edition

ISBN: 978-1-68512-244-7

Cover art by Level Best Designs

This book was professionally typeset on Reedsy.
Find out more at reedsy.com

For Rose – forever and always the one.

Praise for the Nate Ross Novels

"Do you ever wish someone would uncover an unknown Raymond Chandler or Dashiell Hammett—a genuine, hard-boiled novel with gumshoes and molls that has you checking the rounds in your roscoe and flipping pages like a flivver? Well, meet J.R. Sanders's *Bring The Night* starring Nate Ross, a PI with a rhythm and poetry all his own, navigating the City of Angels with clipped wings."—Craig Johnson, author of the Walt Longmire Series

"With a knack for clever turns of phrase and an ability to drop the reader smack-dab in the middle of 1939 Los Angeles, fans of J R Sanders' Nate Ross are in for another time traveling treat with *Bring the Night* that will keep them guessing all the way through this hard-boiled private eye labyrinth."—Martin Turnbull, author *Hollywood's Garden of Allah novels*

"J.R. Sanders' novel (*Dead-Bang Fall*) is a solid addition to L.A.'s noir literary canon. More Nate Ross, please."—Joan Renner, true crime historian, TV commentator, and author (*The First with the Latest!: Aggie Underwood, the Los Angeles Herald, and the Sordid Crimes of a City*)

"The plot (*Stardust Trail*) has more twists and turns than a snorty bronc, taking you through the world of low-budget Westerns and lowlife hoods, down mean streets and into rugged canyons. It's a wild ride, but a fun one all the way."—*Western Way Magazine*

Chapter One

S uicide was all the rage in L.A., the summer of '39. It wasn't the heat; we'd had a mild summer as Southern California summers go. Still, shopkeepers couldn't keep flypaper and rat poison on the shelves. Hardware stores had a run on hemp rope and cheap pistols. And no fewer than five Angelenos so far had made the short hop across the Pasadena line to do gainers off the Colorado bridge.

I was spending a quiet Sunday in the office, where I could handle a few odds and ends without phone calls or other interruptions. Breakfast under my belt and feet on my desk, I was just finishing my second reading of the morning *Times*. I always read it through twice—once for the news and a second time to separate the facts from the horseshit they buried them in to sell copies. I wound it up with the account of the Whitcanack suicide. It made twenty-seven or twenty-eight so far for the season; I'd lost track a few stiffs ago.

Except that he'd chosen the fourth of July, I didn't see anything too imaginative or noteworthy in what seemed like just another run-of-the-mill Dutch act. The guy worked for a downtown travel bureau. The milkman had found him early Friday morning, behind the wheel of a Buick coupe with its engine barely still running in the closed garage of his modest Highland Park home. Cecil J. Whitcanack, forty-three, had booked his own permanent bon voyage and motored straight to his destination without ever putting the car in gear. He was dressed in a white linen suit, his tie was royal blue, and his lips were cherry red. It was a Yankee-doodle-dandy way to go.

What happened to me next was a puzzler. I think eggheads would call

1

it "synchronicity." People who believe in such nonsense might call it "fate." Anyway, as I laid the paper aside, the spring-loaded bell dingus I'd installed over my door a couple weeks earlier, hoping to give the place a more prosperous air, gave out sound. This was the first time anybody'd jingled it but the postman and me. So much for my Sunday solitude.

Two people followed the noise inside: a guy and a girl, twenty-three or so. Clearly related—twins by the look of them. Both had pale, coyote-green eyes, and their hair was an identical shade, so blond it was nearly white. I was pretty sure hers was a wig—going for the Harlow look, maybe—but his was the genuine article. He was on the short side, and she was tall for a girl, which made them about the same height. They were even dressed somewhat alike, in flecked gray tweeds; her skirt suit was slightly mannish, and his three-piece a little foppy. As if he wasn't a strange enough bird, he was sporting a pair of glossy, high-topped shoes of a type I hadn't seen anyone wear since my granddad's day. Congress gaiters, they called them, with elastic sides in place of laces. Maybe he had tender feet. Though his features and hers were startlingly similar, somehow he looked like a soft number, while she looked like anything but. What they didn't look like was heavy money, but I took my feet off the desk anyway.

The young man glanced around like he thought maybe he had the wrong office, but the girl spoke right up in a low, husky voice. "Good morning. Are you Nate Ross?"

"Nate Ross—Investigations" was painted in fake gold leaf on the door's pebbled glass. A brass nameplate on the desk, bought at the same supply house as the door gizmo, also bore my name. If you didn't count a dead cockroach or two, there was no one else in the place but me. Still, some people don't like to jump to conclusions; I can respect that. So I stifled a grin, stood, and politely answered that *yes*, I was indeed Nate Ross.

I usually reserve judgment on people until I've talked to them a little while. But although she'd done no more than ask that one simple question, and before he'd opened his yap at all, I decided that these two were a little on the screwy side. Something about them—I couldn't really say what. Maybe the weird, almost colorless eyes, maybe because they stood too close together.

Maybe it was more than that. Whatever it was, looking at them gave me a sensation like ants were doing a conga line up my backbone.

"How can I help you, miss?" I asked, to move things along. I addressed myself to the girl because she seemed to speak for the pair. If it offended him, he didn't show it.

"I'm Alanna Whitcanack," she said, "And this is my brother, Alan." Matching names, too. Cute.

I smiled and nodded at her, then offered my hand to the boy. It seemed to scare the hell out of him, but he shook it limply with a slender, womanly hand. He even managed to drag out a sort of weak smile.

"Please have a seat," I said, "and tell me what's on your mind." They sat—the girl with confidence, her brother like he suspected a trap. She scooted her chair a little toward his until their knees brushed. It seemed to calm him. It did nothing to ease my case of the willies.

I held up my folded Times. "You're not by any chance related to Cecil Whitcanack?"

He looked ill. She answered crisply, "He was our father."

Synchronicity.

"I'm very sorry," I said, making the requisite solemn face.

"Thank you." She took out a little hanky and dabbed at her eyes. She flicked a glance at her brother, and I sensed that some unspoken message passed between them. He lit a cigarette, handed it to her, then lit one for himself. He took her hand, cleared his throat, and turned dull, dead-fish eyes on me.

"You, uh, know about our father's case, then?" For a kid who didn't seem to practice talking much, he had a smooth voice—not deep, but well-modulated.

I drummed my fingers on the newspaper. "Only what I've just been reading. Is it why you're here?" He gave the girl an uneasy glance. He evidently felt he'd had the floor long enough.

"Yes," she said as she finished wiping her eyes. "You see, whatever the record says, our father did not commit suicide, Mr. Ross. He was murdered."

"Murdered?" I lifted my eyebrows in mock surprise. I'd seen this coming the moment the girl told me her name. Relatives had a tough time accepting a verdict of suicide. Family pride often bucked at the notion. If money came into it, it bucked that much harder. Life insurance companies may cough up when it's murder, but they pay out diddly-do for suicide, and so far, I was betting that was the main, if not only, concern of these two oddballs. Sometimes I hate being so cynical. The trouble is, I keep proving myself right.

"If you had only known our father, Mr. Ross," she went on, "you'd realize that suicide is simply impossible. There's no logical reason for his doing such a terrible thing."

I sat forward and gave her the soft eye. "Yet people do such things every day, Miss Whitcanack," I said in my most soothing tone. "The reasons are always logical to them, I suppose, whatever the rest of us might think."

She pointed a defiant chin at me. "Not father." She mashed her cigarette out in my ashtray for emphasis.

"I understand suicide's a painful thing for any family to accept," I said. She opened her mouth to respond, and I hurried on. "But would you really prefer it to be murder?"

"I'd prefer—we'd prefer—to know the truth, whatever it may be," she said.

I leaned back and doodled with my finger in the dust on my desktop for a few seconds. I could see the gentle approach was wasted on her. "Okay," I said at last. "Let's assume for a moment that you're right. Murder needs a logical reason, too. Logical to the killer, anyway. Do you know of anyone with a motive for killing your father? Is there any evidence that points to murder?"

"Isn't it your job to determine those things?"

"We haven't established that I have a job yet. I take it you're not satisfied with the official police investigation?"

Alan blanched at the word "police." His sister smirked. "We would hardly be here if I were."

I thought it over. It would probably be a simple enough case. If I didn't take it she'd just find somebody else—maybe someone with fewer scruples. "Fair enough, Miss Whitcanack," I said, "but that's where we start. My fee is thirty dollars a day, plus any expenses. I'll give you an itemized bill at the conclusion. I'll need fifty dollars retainer up front. Is that acceptable?"

Alanna didn't bother to consult her brother but, taking her hand from his at last, she fished a money clip from her purse and peeled off two crisp twenties and a ten. It didn't make a dimple in the wad she was carrying. Maybe the twins were more flush than they appeared.

"And is satisfaction guaranteed?" she asked, laying the bills on my desk. I tucked them away and took out my receipt book to save her from asking.

"You're not buying a refrigerator, Miss Whitcanack," I said as I scratched out her receipt. "You'll get your money's worth of work from me, but I can't promise you the results you want. If it's murder, I'll find that out. But if not...."

"It *is* murder."

I didn't argue the point any further. I changed the subject by asking a few basic questions to get me started. Alanna answered every one while her brother sat and looked only mildly interested, dropping in a word or two of his own here and there just so we'd know he hadn't left the room. She explained that Alan lived in an apartment in Hollywood, where he was an assistant at the public library. She was a clerk in the Hall of Records downtown and had a place in Westlake. Both government workers—that made me wonder about the roll she was carrying. Their mother was recently deceased, and I got the idea, though nothing specific was said, that neither of them had been especially fond of the old man. Even more reason for thinking their main interest in his demise revolved around dollar signs.

Alanna asked me to deal directly with her on all case-related matters, and again I watched her brother for any sign of resentment. Nothing. I told her that public offices being closed today, I'd have to wait until the next day to get started. She didn't love the idea, but said she'd appreciate a call as soon as I turned up anything.

Our business concluded for the time being, I walked them to the door. As they went through, she turned abruptly and took a tight grip on my arm. Her weird green eyes bored into mine, and she said, "I really can't thank you enough, Mr. Ross." The gesture, and her intensity, caught me by surprise, so that all I could do in return was give her a closed-lipped smile and a polite nod. I watched them walk shoulder-to-shoulder down the hallway toward the stairs. As they turned to go down, she took his hand again.

Chapter Two

I hit the office early the next morning. I had a couple phone calls to return before I headed out to work on Whitcanack. I'd gotten more than a little behind on answering my messages, since I was back to taking them myself. For a while, I'd had a nice arrangement thanks to my office neighbor, Dr. Van Holten. His dental assistant/receptionist, Nina Bell, had kindly offered to take any messages that came while I was out. To repay the favor, I took her out for an occasional night on the town. After a while, as Nina and her bright little button eyes started growing on me, the nights out became less and less occasional.

Then just when I was getting the notion she might be hearing church bells, and I was trying to decide whether to fish or cut bait—or abandon ship—Nina got word that her father back in Michigan had dropped dead of a heart attack. We had one last night out, and in the morning I drove her to Union Station. A week or so later, I had a letter from her letting me know she'd made Gull Lake safely and was staying on to look after her mother and that it was unlikely she'd be coming back. I hadn't heard from her since. So, for now, anyway, I was back to handling my own messages and eating dinner all by my lonesome. Nate Ross, *el lobo solo*. So it goes.

After taking care of things at the office, I tooled downtown to see if I could get a look at the police report on Whitcanack. The cops weren't generally keen on sharing that sort of thing with private badges, but I had an in, of sorts. Carl Queenan was a captain in Central Homicide. He'd been a lieutenant when we met, and though he was reluctant to own up to it, he owed the promotion partly to me. To my cases, anyway. Still, we'd never been pals exactly, and I doubted we ever would be. But we crossed paths now and then and did each other occasional small favors, so that we were in a sort of constant state of obligation, one to the other. At the moment, he owed me.

Queenan looked up irritably as I rapped on his door frame. He didn't look any happier when he clocked my face.

"Jeez, I skip church one Sunday, and Nate Ross shows up at my door," he grumbled. "The wife said I'd be sorry."

I tried hard to picture Queenan in a church. I wondered if he lost the ever-present cigar, or stubbed it out, at least, before he went inside.

"Come on in and rest the dogs." He slapped a file folder shut and laid it on top of a precarious pile at the corner of his desk, "The sooner you tell me what you want, the sooner I can tell you to go to hell and get back to the city's business."

I took a seat and dropped my hat on his desk. It kicked up a small gust that threatened to topple his stack of case files. He glowered at me and shifted his cigar butt from one corner of his mouth to the other.

"Well, spill it. What brings you around to louse up my Monday?"

"Suicide. Cecil Whitcanack."

"What about it?" I knew he wouldn't even have to think about it. The guy was a walking encyclopedia of his division's cases.

. "Just wanted to ask a couple of things. First, the big one: was it a righteous suicide?"

"As I'm sitting here. Who's tellin' you it ain't?"

I gave him my innocent eyes. "A client. You know I can't say more than that."

"Blah," he said, fanning the air with a hairy mitt. "Save it. Those gold-diggin' twins of his got their spooky green eyes on a boodle of insurance cash if they can make it murder."

"Is there a boodle?"

He took his cigar out, studied the tip. "The guy had a policy. Fifteen grand. Not a fortune, but not short dough either." He replanted the stogie. "Well,

8

boo-hoo for them, 'cause their old man scratched himself, and that's that."

"Anything at all about it ring wrong?"

Queenan shook his head. "Not a thing. Simple and straightforward. I coulda sent a rookie patrolman to handle it." He grinned. "Hell, even a private eye."

"Who *did* you send?"

"You said 'a couple of things.' I answered three questions already. I don't have all day to shoot the lemon with you."

"Last question, I promise."

He pointed the cigar at me like a gun. "All right, if it'll buy me a little peace and quiet. Bill Lockwood took the call." He jabbed the cigar to the left. "Two doors down, left side. But don't come back here weepin' to me if he tells you to jump up your own ass."

"Thanks, Cap." I picked up my hat and walked out.

Two doors down, I stopped in an open doorway and looked around at a small, sparse room with nobody in it. Two desks, both empty, were pushed nose-to-nose in the middle. No nameplates. One had its chair pushed in, and the top cleared of everything but a blotter, a sharpened pencil, and a gooseneck lamp. The other desk's chair sat back and angled toward the open door. A short, neat stack of files sat next to an identical blotter, and an inverted hubcap clearly serving as an ashtray held a burning cigarette. I settled onto the chair next to this desk and fired up a pill of my own.

I hadn't taken more than the first draw before I heard footsteps approaching. They paused briefly at the doorway, then a tall figure brushed past me and dropped into the desk chair. He was about my age or a little younger. Long, wiry build, wavy dark hair, Clark Gable mustache over a mouth twisted to one side in what I guessed was a more or less permanent smirk. Without a word, he picked up the cigarette, took a long pull at it, and shot the smoke out the side of his mouth before turning hard, black eyes on me.

"Sorry," he said. "Had to run to the can. What do you need, Mac?"

"Bill Lockwood?" I asked in a not-unfriendly way.

He tapped ash into the hubcap and inclined his chin a notch for an answer.

I had a card ready and slid it toward him. "The name's Nate Ross, and

9

I'm—"

"I know who you are." He looked at the card like I'd laid a dead rat on his desk. "I've been expecting you."

"Expecting me? How's that?"

He started to slide the card back to me, then checked himself and slipped it into his topdesk drawer. "Not you in particular, but I thought one of you boys would be coming around." He took another drag at his cigarette and grinned at the ceiling. "It's funny, there's what—two dozen private dicks in town? She could have hired any one of 'em."

"She?"

"No need to play foxy, Ross. Whitcanack's green-eyed girl. Maybe both of the twins, but she'd have all the say. I doubt she lets that chicken-brained brother of hers cross the street by himself."

"Sorry, I can't say who my client is."

He grinned. "And you don't need to. She couldn't convince me or the captain to call her old man's suicide a murder, so she's paying you to poke your beak in, am I right?"

"Like I said—"

"Skip it. I don't really care. I'll just ask again: what do you want from me?"

"Just to answer a few questions, if you don't mind."

"And if I *did* mind?"

I got tired of always having to do this dance. "Look, pal, I have a job to do. Maybe you don't like it. Fine. I'm not all that crazy about it myself, but I've agreed to take it on, and I'll see it through whether it gets your nose out of joint or not. I'm not looking to upset anybody's apple cart. So far, it sounds like suicide to me, too, and I've told my client as much. If you want to get me out of your hair, the quickest way you can do that is to give me a little help."

"Easy, Mac. Don't blow a gasket." He gave me the eye for a moment or two, jiggling his cigarette up and down in the corner of his mouth. "Here's the thing. I don't know if you've heard, but we just got a new chief a couple weeks back, and he's shaking things up but good."

I had heard. Art Hohmann was still a sergeant with the city police back when I was on the sheriff's department. I hadn't really known the guy, but if

10

"shaking things up" meant he planned to get rid of all the monkeyshines that had gone on under Jim "Two-Gun" Davis, the new *jefe* had my vote.

"So," Lockwood went on, "That being the case, I'm not too eager to get my tit in a wringer for a private copper I don't know from Adam. I'll have to run this by my captain first. If he wants to okay it, then it's his tit."

"Queenan knows me. It was him sent me over here." He looked surprised. I pointed at his desk phone and added, "Call him if you don't believe me."

He studied me for a moment, then snuffed his cigarette out in the hubcap and dusted his fingers. "No need, I guess. Maybe we can get along. Go on and ask your questions."

I wasn't used to getting anything out of the local cops without a fight. It didn't cut any ice with them that I'd been one of the brotherhood once. I'd testified against a few bad apples among them several years back, and that put me firmly and forever on the other side of the fence with most of the rest. So Lockwood's sudden shift threw me a little.

I tried to hide my surprise as I asked him, "Any clue as to why he did it?"

He shrugged. "His wife died a little less than a year ago. Cancer. He had no other family but the twins, and I'm gonna assume you've met them. Not exactly your warm and cozy family unit."

"He leave a note?"

"More or less." He paused like he was weighing a decision, then slipped one of the files from the stack on his desk. He took out a half sheet of cream-colored paper and slid it over to me. I leaned forward and read it without touching it. It was a page torn from a book—a hymnal from the look of it. Page number 218. Under the title "Awake Ye Saints" and a few bars of music were printed several blocks of lyrics. The last verse had a bold circle inked around it. It read:

"Ye wheels of nature speed your course; ye mortal powers decay;
Fast as ye bring the night of death, ye bring eternal day."

"That was found lying on the front seat next to him," Lockwood said.

"You're figuring it was his notion of a suicide note?"

"What else would it be?"

"He didn't leave any kind of written note at all?"

"No, but that's not unusual in a rum case. Autopsy showed he had a bellyful of whiskey."

"A boozehound?"

He shrugged. "He drank about like the average joe, I guess. No more, no less."

I pointed. "His fingerprints on this paper?"

He shrugged. "Didn't waste the time looking. Coming off a busy night, and the crime scene boys had plenty more urgent calls waiting. I had 'em take a couple photos and sent 'em on their way."

"You find the book it came from?" He hesitated, then shook his head. I asked if I could look at the photos, and he shrugged again, took some glossy snaps out of the folder, and handed them to me. Basic shots of the car interior with broken glass and the hymn book page lying on the front seat. Another shot of the corpse lying on a bed of dry grass in his neat linen suit, looking like the standard monoxide case.

"The body had already been moved," Lockwood said. "The milkman dragged him out onto the lawn, for what good it did. The doc who looked him over at the scene said he'd been dead for several hours. Autopsy narrowed it down to three or four."

"The milkman check out?"

He opened the file and recited in a bored, singsong, let's-get-this-over-with voice, "Robert Hockman, age thirty-seven. He's worked for the dairy for six months. Bachelor, lives in Glassell Park, pays his rent on time. Work record's all right, no arrest record." He looked up at me. "Anything else?"

"You have any beef with me talking to him?"

He closed the file and gave me a meaningless grin. "Why bother to ask? You're gonna do it anyway."

"Yeah, but I figured I should give you the courtesy."

He stared at me before answering. "Well, I get little enough of that in this job. Let's just say I'm okay with it so long as you're not taking anybody for a sleigh ride. I've got no use for the twins, but I won't stand for them being chiseled, either."

"I'm not pulling any stalls. Not my style. Like I told the captain, I've already

12

explained to the client that if it's suicide, it's suicide. Whatever I find, I'll give them square, and as soon as I can."

"All right, then. Do what you need to do—I won't stand in your way." He gathered up the hymnal page and photos, slid them back inside the file folder, and replaced the folder in his pile. "That it?"

I asked a few more questions, scribbled a few notes. "Just one more thing," I said, tucking my notebook away. "What was with the crack about two dozen private dicks?"

"I didn't mean anything by it. It's just that you're famous around here, kind of."

"*Infamous*, you mean."

He raised a hand. "Don't read me wrong, Ross. All that ancient history means squat to me—I've got no use for bent badges myself."

I looked at him for any indication he was giving me the razoo, but saw none. "Okay," I said. "Well, thanks for your time." I stood. "See you around." He nodded, and I went out.

I leaned in Queenan's doorway and tapped on the frame again. He looked up and grimaced.

"Jeez, you still haunting me?"

"Just on my way out."

"I'm happy to hear it. How'd you and Lockwood hit it off?"

"He didn't tell me to jump up my ass."

"Well, look at that—you made a pal. So why you back here botherin' me?"

"You mind if I have a look around Whitcanack's house?" I figured that Lockwood had stuck his neck out as far as he planned to.

"By 'look at,' you mean *toss*." I started to answer, and he hoisted his big paw. "Save your lyin' breath. If I said no, I doubt it'd keep you out. Key's under the back door mat, so don't go bustin' any locks."

"Okay, thanks."

"And don't take nothin'."

I just nodded. When I didn't move to go, he asked, "Somethin' else?"

I wasn't sure I wanted to ask, but I needed to know. "Is there any particular reason your boys used a light touch on this job, Cap?"

"What the hell's that mean?" He leaned forward, like he might come out of his seat. "You questionin' how I run things?"

"No, I know how you run things—that's why I ask. Lockwood seems like a square enough john, but it looks as if he just went through the motions here. No prints, no real follow-up. I don't know the guy, but I know you. Yet you signed off on it."

"That's right, I did." He glowered as he sat back again. "You know, you got a lot of sack waltzin' in here askin' for favors then knockin' our work. What do you think—you're gonna show us up on this one? Nate Ross, the one-man band, gonna teach the big city police force how it's done?"

I held my hands up in mock surrender. "Not trying to. I told Lockwood—I'm just doing a job."

"Uh-huh. You figure if you did make monkeys of us, I'd be afraid to show my face in public, maybe fold up my tent and blow town, is that it?"

"I don't know, Cap. There was a guy once, an English earl or something, back in Queen Elizabeth's day. He made such an embarrassing blunder he took it on the lam and didn't come back home for years. And all this bird had done was break wind in front of the queen."

He squinted at me, snorted a laugh. "Where the hell did you get that yarn?"

"I read it somewhere. I don't exactly recall."

"Well, you can trot out all the fartin' Englishmen you want—it don't make no difference to me." He snatched a file off his stack, flipped it open, and buried his nose in it. "Now, breeze—I'm busy."

14

Chapter Three

W hitcanack's house was one of those small, two-story Craftsman jobs like a thousand others around the area, all river rock and redwood shingles and a front door I could have driven my car through without scraping the jamb. It sat on the canyon's edge midway down a narrow, tree-shaded street that the next hard rain might send sliding, houses and all, over the lip into the Arroyo Seco. The grounds were better kept than I'd have expected for a guy who'd been living the bachelor life for nearly a year. A lot of the grass was brown—not unusual in a Southern California summer—but it was trimmed and edged, and the hedges were neat. The house didn't yet have the look of vacancy but did have the faint air of a place where bad things had happened. Even without what I already knew, it felt like a dead man's house.

I started with the clapboard garage, the scene of the tragedy. It sat to the rear and to one side, at the end of a concrete driveway with a neat grass strip running lengthwise down its center. It had a rolling door on the right, for the car, and a walk-through door on the left. Neither was locked. The walk-through opened into a tool room separated from the garage by an inner wall with another door. Behind the rollaway sat the death car, a dark gray Buick. It was as neat and nondescript as the house and, I suspected, its owner.

The sedan's front driver's side window was smashed in. According to Lockwood, the milkman had done that. He'd found the car locked and running with Whit behind the wheel, passed out or dead. He'd bashed out the window and dragged Whitcanack out into fresh air, then he'd backtracked to the neighbor's house to call for police and an ambulance.

At first look, nothing in the car or garage conflicted with the official call of suicide. No signs of struggle, no blood, nothing out of place, the only drag marks from the car to the back lawn. I took a quick look through the car, careful to avoid disturbing anything. There was broken glass all over the driver's seat and jammed down in the cushions. Both doors were unlocked. I closed the garage back up.

I found the key where Queenan said it would be. The house was hot and stuffy, and despite the fact that the cops had clearly tossed the place it was plain to see that it had been kept as neat as the grounds around it. It didn't seem as though Cecil had done any redecorating since he'd lost his wife. The place had the usual look of a middle-class married couple's home. Lace curtains stretched across the wide windows, doilies protected the living room tables, and feminine knickknacks adorned the built-in bookshelves. In the bedroom upstairs, a vanity stocked with creams and powders pointed to a female presence, as did half a closet full of women's clothing and shoes. A light coating of dust said none of the shoes had been worn in quite some time. Cecil was evidently the sentimental type; he hadn't gotten rid of her things. Now he never would.

The walls and bookshelves in the living room were covered with the usual bric-a-brac of family life. There were photos of the twins as babies, photos of the parents, pictures, and souvenir geegaws from family vacations to Yosemite and the Grand Canyon. Lying flat on one bookshelf was a fairly recent, unframed snapshot of the twins. I pocketed that for my files. On another wall, a tiger oak mantel hung over a fireplace covered in glazed green tiles. A brass urn centered on the mantel was engraved *WHITCANACK*, and on a line below it, *Althea—February 9, 1899 - September 7, 1938*. Hello to the late Mrs. Whitcanack. It was a good-sized urn; I supposed her husband would be joining her in there soon. A framed plaque on the wall above the urn had the twins' small hand prints in plaster of Paris, along with photos of them at four or five years old, wearing matching plaid outfits and posing in front of a Christmas tree. The overall image here was one of a normal, happy, stable family.

A pretty picture, but it didn't quite jibe with my impression of the

Whitcanack twins. If they'd lived a hunky-dory life as kids, what had changed? And why? Or maybe nothing had changed, and this stuff was all for show. You can paint over a wall that's marred and dirty and moldy and make it look fresh and clean and bright. But beneath it, that filthy surface remains, and it only takes a nick in the new paint to show it. It struck me then that most of the time, that's what my job is. I'm the guy who scratches the surface to see what lies underneath.

I'd just started going through desk drawers when a shadow darkened the white curtains across the door glass, and a key rattled in the lock. I scuttled through the swinging door that led into the kitchen. There was just enough space between it and the frame that I could view the front door. It might be one of the Whitcanack twins checking on the place. Maybe not. Either way, odds were I'd learn something by watching unseen.

It was neither twin; it wasn't anyone I recognized. It was a big, rough-looking customer in a crisp blue suit and a shaggy gray nutria fur hat. Fifty or so, with a head that belonged in a Mardi Gras parade, a heavy jaw and pig eyes, and hands like clumps of bananas. He stopped midway across the living room, frowned, and looked all around him. He was sensing, without seeing, that something was out of whack. Only two types of people have that kind of instinct—coppers and crooks. And he didn't carry himself or dress like a cop.

I adjusted my position a little and watched him through the hairline opening. I slid my .380 out, just in case. He stood a moment more, sniffing the air then, apparently satisfied, went directly over to a green upholstered chair with a matching ottoman in the fireplace corner. He sat in the chair, which creaked and popped in protest. He surveyed the room, his big, ugly mug pinched in concentration. After a minute of that, the chair's cushions heaved a sigh of relief as he got up again. He went to the desk I'd been about to pillage and started pawing through drawers and pigeonholes, muttering to himself.

Not finding whatever he was after, he cast an irritated glance around the room and moved toward the stairway. I was shifting to get a better angle when the floorboards gave out a telltale creak. He stopped and swung his big head toward the kitchen. I backstepped quickly to the outer door as I could hear his footsteps approach. I'd never get out without being seen, so I stowed my gun and eased out onto the porch, swung the door half-closed, and took hold of the key in the lock. As the big man came through the swinging door, I made as though I was just entering through the back. His eyes widened, then narrowed, and he shot a hand behind his lapel.

"Easy, friend," I said, palms out towards him. "Burglars don't use keys." His eyes flicked to the key in the lock, then back to my face. His hand stayed where it was.

"Who the hell are you then?" The voice was smoother than I'd have expected from a mug his size. He had the faintest hunky accent.

"I'll ask you the same question," I said, in a more-or-less friendly way. "Since it's a sure bet you're not Cecil Whitcanack."

"Wise boy," he growled, looking me up and down. He evidently wasn't in a friendly mood. He went ahead and showed me the gun—a long, black revolver. "Talk it up, sunshine, before I pop you, or call copper." He smiled, showing me big yellow teeth. "Make any moves, and I'll pop you first, *then* call copper."

I kept my hands out front. Very gently, I took a business card out of my breast pocket. "My name's Ross. I'm a private investigator." That didn't thaw him any. "I'm looking into Whitcanack's death."

"Why for?" He made a sort of question mark in the air with the gun's muzzle. "He croaked himself, didn't he?"

"Probably. But not everyone's convinced."

"Who ain't?"

"I can't say." I waggled the card. "That's the *private* part."

He gave me a disgusted look and stowed the gun. "The Bobbsey twins," he said with a sneer. "Working the murder angle so they can cash in. Ain't that right?"

I shrugged, and he gave me another disgusted look.

I lowered my hands and put the card back in my pocket. "If we're getting along now, you mind telling me now who *you* are, and what you're doing in here?"

"I came in for a drink of water. It's hot out." To convince me, he took a glass from a cabinet and filled it at the tap.

"That's not exactly what I meant."

"I know what you meant, buddy. I may look stupid, but I ain't." He drained the glass and smacked his lips in satisfaction. "The name's Dubek. Charlie Dubek." He waited for a reaction, and seemed to be annoyed when he didn't get it. "Cecil and me were business associates, you could say."

"Close associates, I'm guessing, since you have a key to his house."

He shrugged his massive shoulders. "I live just a mile or so over, up Mount Washington." He motioned with a thumb. "I look in on the place for him whenever he's out of town."

"Looks like he's out of town for good this time."

"Yeah, well, I figured I should make sure the cops locked up tight. I ain't so fond of his kids, but I guess they got a right to their old man's things without some junkie picking the place clean."

"Mighty decent of you."

"I try to be a good neighbor." He refilled his glass, drank it down again. "So what—you here looking for clues?"

"Mostly just trying to get a read on Whitcanack. To see if he was the suicide type."

"Hell, everybody's the type in the right situation," Dubek said.

"What was his situation?"

Dubek shrugged. "His business maybe wasn't so hot. His kids were a disappointment. Wife died a while back. Take your pick."

"He give any clue he might be headed that way?"

"Not to me. But like I say, we was just business associates."

"You in the travel game, too?"

He gave me a close look like he thought I might be putting him on. "Printing. I own a commercial outfit. We do all of his company's printed goods—stationery, business cards, contracts, travel brochures, and whatnot."

"And you see to his house when he's gone. A full-service printer."

His pig eyes screwed down, and he started to say something rough but stopped himself. He took a second to get his face under control before he spoke. "So, you got the case all figured out yet? Suicide, murder, or what?"

"Too soon to tell. This is my first stop."

"But you seem like a bright guy. Bet you got some ideas already, though."

"Maybe. But no answers yet."

He leaned against the counter and gave me what was supposed to look like a friendly smile. "You know, it seems like maybe if the coppers say it's suicide, that oughta be the end of it. No point in soakin' Whit's kids just to end up tellin' 'em what they already been told."

"I'm not soaking anybody, pal. They're paying my rate—which isn't making me rich—to look into this thing. So I'm looking."

"And now you've had a look. So maybe for everybody's good, you should leave it go at that."

"'For everybody's good.' Meaning yours?"

"Meaning yours too, maybe." He showed me the palms of his huge mitts. "Just a friendly word of advice."

I got the feeling he'd been drawing out our little chat, hoping I'd leave the house first. He seemed to catch on that I wasn't going to, so he cut it short. He set his glass on the counter and pushed the swing door half open.

"Well, I guess I can count on you to lock up. So long, pal. Think about it."

He didn't wait for an answer but went through the doorway and out through the front door. I went to the living room window and watched him climb into a shiny black Cadillac parked in front of the neighbor's house. He drove off without looking my way.

I went back to searching the living room, starting with the desk. As I searched, I tried to decide whether Dubek had bought my back door act or whether he suspected I'd seen him searching.

There was an old pump organ along the wall opposite the fireplace. The stool was one of those oblong bench types with a hinged seat that covered a storage compartment for sheet music. My Aunt Dotty had one just like it. Inside it, I found a stack of sheet music, all gospel stuff. Alanna had told me her mother was a church organist. There were also a couple of hymnals. I flipped through those—both had their pages 218 intact. There was nothing else in the bench. Whatever Charlie Dubek had been looking for, I doubted it was church music.

After an hour of sifting through the place, I didn't come across anything else of interest, so I put out the lights, locked the doors, and replaced the key where I'd found it. I fetched my print kit from the trunk of my car and dusted Whitcanack's Buick, mainly the steering wheel and starter. Nothing. I tried a few other spots where there should have been prints, but there weren't any. Somebody, it seemed, had done a wipe job. I didn't like that.

As I drove away, I thought over my talk with Dubek. Ideas, I had all right. Now it was time to go after a few answers.

I drove back to the office from Whitcanack's house. I had more stops I wanted to make, but first, I put in a call to Alanna Whitcanack. She was working, so I phoned the Hall of Records and reached her with a minimum of fuss.

"Nate Ross, here. Can you talk for a couple of minutes?"

"Yes, of course. Has something happened?"

"No. You asked to be kept up to date. I've reviewed the police file, and I've been to your father's house. Nothing's for sure yet, but I do have some doubt that your father killed himself."

"Do you have an idea what *did* happen?"

"Too early for that. There's a lot I don't know yet. It all takes time."

"What *can* you tell me? What doubts?"

"To start with, I didn't find any fingerprints on the steering wheel in the car. Suicide or not, there ought to have been something, but it almost looks as if someone wiped them."

There was a long silence, and I wondered if maybe the details were too much for her. "Are you sure you want to know these things?"

"Yes. I'd like to know everything."

I debated telling her about Dubek, but I wanted to find out a little bit about the guy first. "All right," I said. "First—how much did the police already tell you?"

"Not a great deal. Just the basic facts. The milkman found Father in his car with the engine running. No signs of foul play. He left a sort of note."

"Did they show you the note, or tell you what it said?"

21

"Not really."

"It's a page torn from a book. A book of hymns. Does that say anything to you?"

"No, not really. Mother had several hymnals, of course. Why would they think it was a suicide note?"

"It had some lyrics circled—something about bringing the night of death, eternal day, and so on. Does that mean anything to you?"

"Not at all. So what will you do next?"

"I'm going to go see your father's boss, just for some background on your father. Sometimes co-workers know or see things others don't. Then I'm going to talk to Hockman, the milkman who found your father, see if I can get more detail from him than what's in the reports. I'll be in touch."

Chapter Four

The Global Travel Bureau was on the fifth floor of the Pacific Mutual Building at 6th and Grand. Judging by the address and trappings, it was more than a going concern, so I didn't know what to make of Charlie Dubek's claim that Whitcanack's business wasn't so hot. The receptionist put on a grave face and teared up when I stated my business. I took that to mean Whitcanack was well thought of here, at least by her. When she called the agency's manager, he told her to show me right in.

Herman Bausch was a cheerful, ruddy-faced guy in his early fifties. His open blazer showed off the telltale paunch of a career desk-sitter. "Awful deal. Just awful," he said with a mournful look as we settled in on opposite sides of his desk. "Whit was a real square egg. You're working for his kids, I suppose."

I was getting tired of denying it. Still, I didn't exactly admit it, either. "Just looking for a little more...clarity, I guess you could say, than the official investigation offered."

He just pursed his lips and nodded.

"How long had he worked for you, Mr. Bausch?"

"Herm, call me Herm. Oh, let's see...." He scratched his sizable bald spot and tallied in the air. "Six, no seven years. Seven years in May." He reddened. "This past May, that is, not...well, you know."

"And what exactly was his job here?"

He gave me an indulgent smile. "Well, we're travel agents. Nation-wide and worldwide, just like the name says," he added with pride. His voice shifted to salesman-ese. "Whether you want to go to Budapest, Bangkok, or Bali, or anywhere in the States, from Portland, Oregon to Portland, Maine, we're your guys."

"No, I get that. What I mean is, what were his specific duties? What would a typical day at work be for Cecil Whitcanack?"

"Oh, that." He looked disappointed that I didn't enjoy his spiel. "Well, a big part of it would be meeting with clients to assess their wants and needs. Helping with passports and such if they're traveling abroad and need help. The rest he'd spend arranging rail and airplane travel, hotels, tours, and whatnot, and haggling for the best prices for all that."

"Did he solicit these clients?"

"No, for the most part they're walk-ins, or referrals. That's where the bulk of our trade comes from—referrals. It's a very word-of-mouth business. We don't do much in the way of outside sales. With a guy like Whit, we didn't need to."

"Meaning?"

"He attracted a lot of referrals. An awful lot. His commissions were typically twenty percent or more above my other agents'."

"Really? What was his secret?"

"Don't know. Didn't care, to be honest. It's a competitive game—we're not the only party in town. And I don't need to tell you it's a tough economy. So if Whit could rope in extra trade that might have gone to another agency, it was okey-doke with me. Gift horses and so on."

"I see your point. Looking back on it, was there anything you saw, or he said, that might have pointed to him taking his own life?"

"His wife died not too long ago. But he seemed to be handling that all right. As well as anybody could."

"Anything about him ever give you cause for concern? Anything that seemed a little off?"

His cheery manner slipped a notch or two.

"Something?"

He shifted in his seat, like his piles were bothering him. "Well, I don't like to tell tales on a guy...."

"He'd dead, Herm."

"Yeah. Yeah. Well, there was one thing. I wouldn't say it was *off*, just maybe a little peculiar. He didn't get much repeat business. And that's unusual in our game—satisfied customers tend to come back year after year."

"Ever talk to him about it?"

"No, I never saw the need. Like I say, he brought in more than his share of business from referrals."

"So no idea why his clients didn't come back?"

"None at all. Maybe Lila would have a guess."

"Lila?"

"Lila Porter, his assistant. They were…well, that's not my place to talk about."

"Is she here today?"

"Sure." He picked up his phone.

Lila Porter wasn't the girl I'd have pictured with a guy like Cecil Whitcanack, if that's what Bausch was getting at. Quite a bit younger, for one thing—she couldn't have been much over thirty. Her hair was red, shot through with gold when the light hit just right, and her wide eyes were a smoky blue-gray. Her clothes were a little stylish for office work, but a gunny sack wouldn't have done her figure any harm. She was what the boys with their heels hooked on a brass rail would call "a tomato." Why she'd hitched herself to a middle-aged milquetoast like Whitcanack, if she had, was a mystery. Or maybe it wasn't.

She was carrying a little clutch bag, and I wondered if I'd caught her on her way out to lunch. She looked at me for a good five seconds before she spoke. She was close enough that I could see she also had sparks of gold in her irises. They gave the blue-gray eyes a smoldering look, like warm coals that might flare up at the least disturbance in the air. The ember eyes studied me closely, weighing, judging.

"Mr. Ross." The voice was as smoky as the eyes. "Mr. Bausch said you wanted to speak with me. He didn't say why."

"Please have a seat." Bausch had set us up in one of their consultation rooms. We took chairs at right angles to each other, with a little low table in between. I handed her a business card. She read it with veiled distaste but didn't hand it back. "I've been asked to look into Cecil Whitcanack's death," I said in my gentlest tone.

She paled a bit, but the eyes met mine and held steady. "Yes?"

"Yes. And I was hoping you could answer just a few questions."

She fished a cigarette and matches out of the little clutch, slipping my card inside. Nice steady hands. She looked up at me, and I took the matchbook. I lit her smoke, and she thanked me with a nod.

"I'm afraid I don't quite follow," she said after a dainty puff. "I understood from the police that Whit —" She broke off with a pained look that flickered and died. "That Cecil took his own life. Should I assume that that's not the case? Or at least that someone thinks it's not?"

I fired up a cigarette of my own. To hell with it. "I guess I'm not giving much away," I said, "if I tell you that Mr. Whitcanack's children have some doubts."

"Of course." She blew a contemptuous stream of smoke at the ceiling. Her eyes went cold. "What is it you want from me?"

"Well, to start with…I don't mean to be indelicate, but I've been given the impression that you and Mr. Whitcanack may have been something other than just co-workers. Was that the case?"

If I thought she'd be angry or embarrassed, I'd misjudged her. She blew more smoke at the ceiling, and her mouth turned up at one corner. It was meant to be a sneer, but on her, it raised my temperature a degree or two.

"We'd been seeing each other for several months, if it's any of your business."

"I'm a private detective, Miss Porter. Nothing's any of my business."

That got a genuine smile—a small one. She nodded. "Fair enough. All right, to be frank, we were engaged to be married. I'm surprised his daughter hasn't already mentioned that to you. Surely I'm on her list of suspects."

I ignored the last statement. But I was likewise surprised that Alanna hadn't mentioned Lila Porter. "I get the idea that he and his children were not especially close."

"To put it mildly."

"Well, then," I said to change the subject, "you're probably in the best position to tell me something about his state of mind. Whether he would have had a reason for taking his own life. Whether there were any hints he was considering it."

"I thought you just said there were doubts."

"There are. But it was obviously either suicide or…well, or murder, and it's my job to find out which."

Her eyes widened just a bit at "murder," but she kept her poise. "I see." She used a little more tobacco and sat looking at nothing for several seconds before she spoke again. "I can't imagine anyone wanting to harm Whit. He was a nice, gentle, ordinary man. As for suicide? I assume you know he was a recent widower."

I nodded.

"He and Althea married right out of school, and…." She gave me a close look. "Have you ever lost a loved one, Mr. Ross?"

"I have."

"Then I'm sure you know that whatever the relationship, it leaves a hollowness inside you that nothing—no one—can ever completely fill. I was under no illusions about that with Whit. I tried. But two months ago, he broke our engagement. He wouldn't really give me a reason except to say that it wasn't fair to ask me to share his burdens. I took that to mean the void in him was just too great. So as much as I might like to think otherwise, yes, I do believe it's possible that it overwhelmed him to the point that he saw no other way to rid himself of it. I don't know if that helps."

She'd held back tears, but her voice had gotten thicker the more she said. I gave her a few moments of silence before I said anything. "I appreciate your honesty, Miss Porter. I know this isn't a pleasant matter to discuss, especially with a stranger, and I'm sorry to have to ask you these things."

She looked at her hands. "It's really all right. I'm happy to help find the truth if I can."

"Thank you. If you don't mind, I have a couple questions about Cecil's work here."

She nodded.

"Mr. Bausch said that Cecil brought in more clients than anyone here, both referrals and walk-ins, but that he had very little return business. Is that right?"

"I suppose it is." I sensed a change, a sort of battening down of the hatches. She took a deep drag on her cigarette.

"Do you have any notion why that would be?"

She blew more smoke at the ceiling. "No."

I knew that was either not the right answer or not the whole answer but decided not to press her on it for the time being. "What sort of clients did he have?"

She didn't even attempt to hide her irritation. "All sorts. Our fees are very reasonable, so it's not just the well-to-do who come to us."

"Has business been generally good?"

"Considering the economy, yes. Tourism in Europe has dropped off, naturally, with the situation over there. But otherwise, we've stayed very busy." She mashed her cigarette out in the ashtray, and I recognized my cue.

Women were hard to figure. She'd opened up on her personal dealings with Whitcanack but, for some reason, pulled down the curtain when it came to matters of business. I could see there wasn't any more I was going to get from her just then, so I snuffed out my own cigarette and picked up my hat.

"Well, thanks for talking with me, Miss Porter."

She turned at the doorway like she was about to say something more. Instead, she just gave me a curt nod and walked out.

Doc Reese was holding a brain when I walked into his inner sanctum. Cradling it in both hands, like a newborn baby. He dropped it onto the steel tray above the scale with a wet plop, then mumbled to himself and scribbled a couple of notes on a clipboard. His head came around then like he'd just noticed me.

"Hiya, kid. Been a dog's age." Snapping off his rubber gloves and shoving them into a lab coat pocket, he crossed the room and stuck out a hand.

"Good to see you, Doc." As we shook, I marveled at how strong his grip was—the guy had to be closing in on eighty. Those nimble fingers had been making canoes out of corpses for the coroner's office for well over forty years.

I'd called ahead and told him I was coming, so I knew the bit with the brain was, for my benefit, his idea of a joke. Doc enjoyed making visitors queasy with the sights, sounds, and smells in his little chamber of horrors. The first time I'd ever been there, I was a fresh-faced kid, wearing a shiny new county star, and I'd been sent to pick up an autopsy report for the homicide dicks. I'd found Doc sitting on the steel table beside a badly decomposed "floater" fished from the L.A. River and eating a big bowl of cottage cheese. I was younger then, and he'd gotten the desired effect—my face had gone as green as my uniform, and I'd beat a hasty retreat.

This time around, I was a little more seasoned, and he looked disappointed that he hadn't sent me running for the john. We spent a little time catching up, then I explained why I'd come.

"Whitcanack, eh?" He didn't say anything more, just grinned and watched me with foxy eyes behind his round glasses. I took the cue and held out the offering.

"Come to Papa!" He seized the box and broke the seal. Lifting the lid, he gave the contents a long, satisfied sniff. He flashed me another grin. "Ahh...music to my nose."

I could always buy a favor or two from Doc for a box of El Wadoras, possibly the worst cigars ever made. Two for a nickel at any corner drugstore. I wished all my help came as cheap.

He fired up one of the foul panatelas—he knew better than to offer me one—and took a couple of appreciative puffs. It smelled worse than anything else in the place, and there was some unhealthy competition.

"So," he said, laying the reeking thing on the edge of a counter top, "What exactly do you need to know? He's already been ferried off to the mortuary in case you were counting on a peek."

"Nope, no need. Just got a couple of quick questions."

"I hope you're not trying to turn the cops' suicide into a homicide. That's a sure way to lose friends downtown."

"Lucky for me, I've got none to lose."

He shook his head. "You never did know what was good for you, Nate.

Well, spit it out—what's on your mind?"

"Anything so far that would make you think maybe it *wasn't* a suicide?"

"Of course not, or I wouldn't have ruled it one."

"I saw the report. He was drunk?"

"As a councilman."

"Anything unusual in that?"

"Judging by his liver, I wouldn't say he was a heavy drinker. But a man about to commit suicide is apt to put a few more away than normal."

"You find any broken glass on him? Clothes, hair, anywhere?"

His eyes narrowed. "None." He started to ask a question, but I headed him off.

"I don't suppose he was wearing gloves, by any chance?"

He looked at me over the tops of his specs. "Gloves? In July? Why would you think that?"

"I couldn't find a single fingerprint on the steering wheel, or anywhere else in his car for that matter. So I figure either he wore gloves or else somebody's wiped it."

He grinned again. This time an irritating, I-know-something-you-don't-know kind of grin. "Gloves or not, you wouldn't find this gent's prints. He didn't have any."

"Any what?"

"Fingerprints. Normally they're printed when they're brought in here. But not Whitcanack. Couldn't—his digit tips were smooth as a baby's backside."

"You mean he had them removed, like Dillinger?"

He gave a dismissive wave of the hand. "That's a lot of newspaper hooey, about Dillinger. Oh, he tried to erase them with some sort of lye concoction, but it didn't work. It was his prints that helped identify his body after those agents turned it into a tea strainer. As a matter of fact—"

"Let's save Dillinger for another day," I cut in. Doc was always chock full of facts and eager to share them, but once he got off the topic at hand, it could be hard to steer him back. "What about Whitcanack?"

"I found nothing to indicate he'd tried anything of the kind. No burn or surgical scarring. Offhand, I'd say he was born without them."

"That's possible?"

"It is. Very rare, but entirely possible. There's a doctor over in Europe—the name escapes me—who's doing research on it." He started toward his cluttered desk. "I probably have his journal article here somewhere if you want to take a look."

"Skip it. It'd be way over my head. So would a guy like that leave any kind of marks at all?"

"Well, he still had the usual sweat glands, oils in the skin, and so forth. Most likely, you'd find some blotches, elliptical like normal fingerprints, but blank. No patterns. Did you see anything like that?"

"No, nothing at all."

"And no other prints, you say?" He went thoughtful. He rubbed his chin, then picked up the cigar and took another draw, blew out a cloud of poison gas. "I'd wager your other guess is right, then. The prints were wiped away. And if that's so it's maybe sounding a little less like a suicide."

Chapter Five

I rapped on the frame of the torn screen door. It rattled against the safety hook, giving each knock its own separate echo. It made me sound more urgent than I'd intended. After three or four rounds of this, I heard an irritated voice from inside. "Awright, awright. Keep your shirt on, will ya? Jeez!" The inner door was jerked open, and a guy looked out. Medium height and blocky, wearing work pants, dirty white socks, and a grubby undershirt. His gray-streaked brown hair poked out at odd angles, and he had light brows over watery blue, bloodshot eyes. Watchful eyes. Con's eyes. He rubbed sleep out of them and ran them over me with a baleful stare.

"Bob Hockman?"

His eyes shifted from me to the street beyond, then back. "Whatever you're sellin', bud, I don't need any. I work mornings, sleep afternoons, so I ain't in no mood right now to listen to a sales pitch."

"Sorry to wake you," I said. "I guess I should have thought of your schedule, milkman and all. But I'm not selling anything."

He squinted and raked fingers through his unkempt hair. "I'll bite," he said with a smirk. "Who the hell'd you say you were?"

I pressed a card against the screen, and he squinted harder. "Private investigator?" He looked from the card to me, then back at the card, like maybe he'd missed something. "Whatta you want with me?"

"I'm following up on Cecil Whitcanack's death." That didn't make him look any cheerier. "Just got a few questions, if you wouldn't mind."

He gave me a red-eyed stare for a couple of moments, then unhooked the screen. "Why not? I'm awake now, anyhow. C'mon in."

I followed him through a short hallway and into a dingy, cluttered living room. It looked like it'd last been cleaned about the time I was learning my ABCs and had only gotten a lick and a promise then. He waved me to a ratty sofa, and I took a seat.

"You want a beer?" Before I could answer, he disappeared into the kitchen. He came back with a couple of cans and passed me one. Maier's Select. The kind of stuff a wise man would only *select* to pour down the drain. It was lukewarm and tasted like dog slobber, but I sipped at it to be sociable. I needed answers.

He dropped into a worn, greasy leather armchair. "So," he said after sucking at his own beer, "You're workin' for the family, I guess?"

I just shrugged.

"Gotcha, bud." He winked. "So what can I tell you I ain't already give to the cops?"

"Maybe nothing. I'd just rather get the story straight from the source."

He gave me a suspicious look. "Okay, then, shoot."

I faked another sip of beer. "You were making a milk delivery at Whitcanack's house last Tuesday, dropping off at the back porch, right?" Hockman nodded. "So talk me through it from there."

He took a slug, wiped foam from the corner of his mouth with a thumb. "Awright. I'm settin' down the jugs, lookin' for empties, but they ain't been left out. I hear a car runnin', rough like. Sorta muffled. Comin' from the garage, but the doors are shut. That strikes me as queer, so I roll open the door, and there sits the car, runnin' all right. Tough to see anything for all the smoke. I pull the light cord, and that's when I lamp the guy, kinda slumped over behind the wheel. The car's locked up, so I bang on the window, but this bird's out—I mean *out.*"

He paused for another go at his beer. "Can't hardly breathe in there for the fumes. I figure I gotta do something, quick. There's a pipe wrench on the workbench, so I grab it and bust out the window. I drag the guy out onto the lawn, away from the garage. I see it's Whitcanack, the guy who lives there. He's stinkin' of hooch, and he don't look so good. Face like a ghost, lips red as a two-dollar whore's, not breathing. I figure he's gone but, hell, I ain't no doctor. So I leave him there and go wake up the next-door neighbor to put in a call." He drank more beer. "That's about it."

"What time was this?"

"When I got there? Five-fifteen, five-thirty."

"You touch anything in the car?"

"Only to shut off the motor." He gave the answer a little too quick for me.

"See anything else in the car?"

"Like what, for instance?"

"Anything that didn't look like it belonged there?"

"No. I mean, there was a paper on the seat, printing on it, but I didn't pay it any mind. Anyhow, the cops took that."

"Speaking of cops, how long was it before they showed up?"

"After the neighbor called? Ten minutes or so. A couple of prowlies and an ambulance right behind 'em. Detective showed up maybe half an hour after that. Lockhart, or somethin' like that."

"So long enough, then."

"Long enough for what?"

"For you to cook up a story they'd buy."

He stopped in mid-sip. "How's that again?"

I smiled. "The coppers don't mind if you bend the truth a little here and there, Bob. They expect it. But flat-out lies will get you jammed up with 'em every time."

He plunked his beer down on the side table, slopped some of it over. "What the hell are you drivin' at? Lies about what?"

"For instance, you didn't tell 'em he was in the passenger seat when you found him, not the driver's."

He paled a little. He tried to cover with a belligerent front, puffing up like a bullfrog. "Who says he was?"

"I do." He leaned forward, fists knotted, and I held up a warning hand. "So does the broken glass I found wedged in the driver's seat cushions. It didn't get there if he was sitting in that seat when you busted out the window. And if he was behind the wheel, how the hell did he not get glass in his hair and clothes?"

Hockman's hands unclenched. He leaned back, took a sudden interest in his stocking feet, and puckered his lips in and out a few times. It seemed to deflate him. Finally, he squinted up at me.

"You're a private badge, right?"

"What of it?"

"Meaning what I tell you, you don't have to tell the cops."

"That all depends," I said. "If you tell me you cut your milk with chalk dust, that's one thing. Tell me it was you that bumped off Thelma Todd, that's something else."

"And where would jumping parole, say, land on that scale?"

"The cops told me your record's clean. How's that if you're on parole?"

"I ain't." He looked behind him and side to side, as though there might be someone around to overhear. He dropped his voice to a con's murmur. "That is, *Bob Hockman* ain't, if you get me."

"I get you. So what's your real name, rank, and serial number?"

"Uh-uh, brother. Not until I know you'll keep it under the hat, if then."

"Fine, fine, later for that. Just give me whatever you left out with the cops, or anything you did tell them that wasn't strictly on the square."

"I mostly gave 'em the straight dope. Except, like you say, the guy bein' on the wrong side. That got me worried some. A guy in my shoes can't get tangled up in no homicide cases. I figured what's the diff, anyhow? Murdered or not, he's just as dead."

"And...?" They never gave you everything on the first run. He shrugged and gave me innocent eyes. "Why'd you wipe the car?"

"Aw, bud..."

"You want me to keep your little secret, or not?"

He sat back with an aggrieved sigh. "Like I said, I smelled murder. I figured if there wasn't no evidence to fool around with, they'd for sure write it off as a Dutch. That way, I don't get pulled into court as no witness."

"You get rid of anything but prints?"

His eyes wobbled. "Nah, nothin'."

"You bullshit me, *Bob*, and our deal's off."

"You got a hard crust on you, mister," he whined. "Okay, okay. Look. There was a bottle, that's all. On the floorboard, driver's side. A fifth of Ten High, three-quarters empty."

"What happened to it?"

"I finished it. I was feelin' a little shaky by then, and old Whitcanack sure as hell didn't need it no more. I figured, if anything, the coppers would just dump it in the grass or use it themselves."

"What did you do with the empty?"

"Put it in the trash barrel, side of the garage."

"You wipe it, too?"

The flash of fear in his eyes said he hadn't. He swore under his breath.

"Don't sweat it," I said. "But I'm gonna need to take your fingerprints, to count you out."

He threw up both hands. "Nothin' doin', pal. I give you plenty already—you ain't gettin' my prints." I started to argue but decided it would get me nowhere.

"All right, forget it." I stood and took out my handkerchief, pretended to wipe a little spilled beer off my hand. "You sure you've told me everything? That's it?"

He bobbed his head several times. Too many times, I thought. But I had enough for now, and I wanted to get back to the house and find that bottle, if it was still there.

"Okay then," I said. "Thanks for the info, and the beer." I leaned over and, using the handkerchief, snatched his beer can from the table.

I dropped a card where the can had been. "If you think of anything you forgot..."

"You son of a bitch!" He got up and followed me to the door. "Don't you screw me on this deal. Do me right, brother."

"That's up to you, pal."

"I did just remember one other thing," he said as I walked out. "I'm still owed three bucks on that bird's account." He shouted through the screen after me. "I guess I ain't gonna get it now!"

I shook the last of the beer out on the dead grass as I walked away.

I headed up Figueroa from 3rd, back toward Highland Park and Whitcanack's house. I could recall seeing a tin trash barrel between the side of the garage and the fence. As I drove, I thought over Hockman's story, wondering how much was true and how much was bullshit. Under the circumstances, I didn't see him as a suspect, but I knew better than to believe half of what a con told me.

The late afternoon traffic was heavy, and as I wound my way through it, I noticed that a blue Chevrolet with a gray rag top about four cars back seemed to be pacing me. I was almost certain I'd seen the same car parked down the street from Hockman's. I sped up as I hit the tunnels, and the Chevy stayed with me. After the river, I made a quick right onto one of the avenues and zigzagged through a few residential streets. When I'd wended my way back onto Figueroa, I didn't see the convertible anywhere.

The house looked just as I'd left it earlier. I'd been a little concerned Dubek might return after I left, but I figured if he did, he did. It wasn't like I could set up camp on the place.

I had no trouble finding Hockman's bottle. It was lying on its side on top of the pile of assorted refuse that half-filled the barrel. I stuck a pencil down the bottle's neck, carefully lifted it out, and took it to my car. I laid it on the rug in the trunk. It would be getting dark soon, and I'd spent enough time here, so I'd take the bottle back to the office and print it there. On the drive back, I kept one eye on the mirror but didn't see any sign of the blue Chevy.

Back at the office, I had second thoughts. I hadn't eaten for a good part of the day, and my stomach was complaining. Checking the bottle for fingerprints could wait; I'd have nothing to compare them to but Hockman's, even if I did find any. I locked the bottle in my desk and made a note to visit the coroner's office in the morning to see if I could smooth-talk my way into a copy of Cecil Whitcanack's prints.

Meanwhile, I called downstairs to Gus's Diner and asked Gus's nephew Benjy to bring me up a roast beef sandwich and some potato salad. While I waited, I dialed Alanna Whitcanack's home phone number. She answered on the second ring, and we arranged that I'd drop by the next day to let her know where things stood.

Half an hour later, stomach pacified, I decided to enjoy a quiet cigar before calling it a day. Fishing in my pocket, I found Lila Porter's matchbook. I must have stuck it there after lighting her smoke. It was from the Biltmore Hotel, next block over from Global Travel Bureau. I didn't peg her as a roundheels, but the Biltmore had one of the classiest bars in town, and that did fit her. I'd been contemplating a drink anyway, so I thought it was worth taking a chance.

I spotted her right away, sitting alone at a corner table and frowning over a cocktail glass. She didn't even look up as I walked past, but I still did a half-convincing double take before backstepping to her table.

"Miss Porter?"

She looked up, a little startled, as though she'd been caught doing something she wasn't supposed to. When she registered the face, she forced a polite smile.

"Mr. Ross. I wouldn't have expected to see you here."

"A little too seedy to fit in?"

She turned a charming shade of red. "Not at all. I didn't mean… It's just that this place is a little…froufrou."

"Is it?" I looked around with mock appraisal. "And I'm not?"

The red faded, and she gave a nervous laugh. "Hardly."

"I guess that's a compliment." I gave her the disarming Nate Ross smile. "Maybe."

A red-jacketed waiter materialized next to me. "Drink, sir?"

"Oh, no, I'm not—"

"Join me, please." She gestured to the chair across from her. "I could use a little conversation."

"All right." I took a seat and set my hat on the chair beside me. I looked at her glass. "What are you having?"

"Gin Rickey."

I tried not to make a face. "Double bourbon, no ice," I told the waiter. He floated off, and she sipped her drink and watched him go.

"Not a fan, I take it?"

"Never had a stomach for gin. I think it's the smell. Reminds me of witch hazel."

Her eyes smiled at me over the rim of her glass. "I'll try and stay downwind." The cool gray eyes studied me. "It's not a coincidence, is it, Mr. Ross? Your turning up here?"

"It's Nate," I said. "And no, not exactly." I reached into my pocket. "I needed to return your property."

The waiter reappeared and set my bourbon down. When he left again, I slid the matchbook across the table.

Her eyebrows arched, and she gave me a knowing smile. "You *are* aware that they give those away here? Free of charge."

"Is that so? See, the kind of places where guys like me drink, they even charge you for the ice." I tasted the bourbon. "It's one reason I drink mine without the rocks."

That almost got a laugh. "I may have misjudged you, Mr.—Nate. I wasn't imagining you with a sense of humor."

"My mother never thought I was very funny."

"Do mothers ever?" Her face went serious. "I want to apologize for being so rude to you earlier."

"No harm done. I've grown a pretty tough hide."

"I suppose in your line of work, you've had to." She turned her glass on the table, studied the wet ring it made on the cloth. "I've never met a private detective before. Do you carry a gun and everything?"

"Most of the time."

Now she made a face. "I don't like guns."

"I'm not very fond of them myself."

"Then why do you carry one?"

"For the same reason a pilot carries a parachute. Because if you get in a jam where you need one and don't have it, odds are you'll never need one again."

She thought that over. "Have you always been a detective?"

"Well, not right from the cradle, but...." I took another sip and decided I should dispense with the wisecracks. "Sorry, bad habit. For about five years now. I was a sheriff's deputy before that."

"Here in Los Angeles?" I nodded. "It didn't suit you?"

"It may be that I didn't suit it." I didn't often spend time in the company of women like Lila Porter. I wasn't going to waste any of it telling sob stories. "How long have you worked for the travel agency?"

She paused at the change of subject but took the hint. "It'll be three years next month. I worked at another agency before that, but the boss there... Well, let's just say he expected me to put in *extra hours*."

"Do you enjoy your work now?"

"I do, mostly. There's always an element of envy, though, when you work in travel. You spend your days planning exciting, exotic vacations for other people—trips that time and circumstance won't allow you to take for yourself."

"I guess I can understand that."

"You guess?"

"I'm pretty much a homebody. There's not much of the wanderlust in me."

"Have you never traveled at all?"

"I've been to Santa Barbara a couple of times."

That prompted a genuine laugh. It made her eyes sparkle, and I saw the flecks of gold again. She took a healthy swallow of gin. "Are you married?" There seemed to be a little edge to the question.

"I was. I'm not anymore. And you?" It was out before I thought about it.

"Almost."

"Of course. I'm sorry."

She waved the apology away. "Don't be. But that is really why you're here, isn't it? More questions about Whit?"

"Well—"

"I don't mind, Nate. As I said before, if I can help, I will."

"Okay." I took a deep swallow of bourbon. "Okay. I wonder how well you know his kids, if at all."

She finished her drink, and I signaled the waiter for another.

"I've only seen them one time. It was plain the daughter detested me. I suppose I can understand that, although please believe me when I tell you there was nothing between Whit and me while his wife was alive."

"I believe you."

"With the son, Alan, it was as though he couldn't acknowledge my existence. He didn't speak to me at all—even when we were introduced, he just nodded. Whit was always very reticent about his children, rarely spoke of them at work, or to me. But I sensed there was bad blood between him and Alan. With Alanna, there was just a…distance."

"I don't mean to get too personal, but you said when he broke off the engagement, he gave you a vague sort of reason. Did he give you any indication beforehand that that was coming?"

The gray eyes took on an inward look as she considered the question. "Something had changed. A few days earlier, he came into the office in a strange mood. Brooding, distant. I tried to get him to tell me what was wrong, but he insisted that there was nothing to tell."

"And after the break? It must have been uncomfortable, the two of you working together, seeing each other all day, every day."

"It was for me. Whit seemed almost lighter. I really wasn't sure how to take that."

I didn't want to dig any deeper into her painful memories. I wasn't sure there was anything in there that would help me anyway. I thought it might be a safe time to pick up where we'd left off at her office. She'd seemed not to want to talk about Whitcanack's business then, and I had to wonder why. I'd seen by now that she was no fool. With people like her, sometimes the direct approach was best. Sometimes it blew up in your face. I decided to roll the dice.

"When we talked before," I said, "I was asking about Whit's clients and the fact that Herm Bausch said he didn't get a lot of repeats."

She took a drink and leaned back with a rueful smile. "I was wondering when you'd get around to that." I started to speak, but she went on. "I know I was a little evasive. But you were just a man who'd barged in asking questions. I wasn't sure whether to trust you."

"And now?"

"As I said, I can see I misjudged you, and now I'm sorry I did. I can't tell you why he didn't get repeat business because I don't know. Honestly, I don't. But I can tell you what I saw, for what it's worth."

"I'll settle for that."

"Some—many, actually—of Whit's clients were..." She held up a hand. "Understand, I don't know this for certain. It's just an impression I had."

"Okay."

"Quite a few of Whit's clients struck me as shady. I got the impression that they were...I can't think of a nicer term than 'mobsters.' And he always handled those clients' arrangements personally—I was never involved."

"Uh-huh." She gave me a close look, expecting more reaction than that. But when someone's opening up, it's generally better to keep your hash trap shut and let them talk. She didn't say anything more, though, so I was forced to ask. "Did you ever remark on that to him, ask him about it?"

"I did once, in a sort of joking way."

"And what did he say?"

"He just said that even Al Capone took vacations. He said it in a facetious way, too, but the message seemed clear that it wasn't something he wanted to talk about."

"And when was this?"

"Oh, a year and a half ago. Maybe a little longer."

"Did that concern you at all? I mean, you were—" I caught myself. I didn't want to say something I'd kick myself in the ass for later.

"I was going to marry him." I started to answer, to try and dig myself out, but she stayed me with a hand. "I don't blame you for thinking it, Nate. I've thought the same myself. I just ask you to understand. It's so much easier for you, as a man. You have choices that I don't have. Maybe one day, but...."

She swiped a tear away with a knuckle. "I didn't have any great, burning passion for Whit. That sounds awful, I know, but there it is. I just wanted security, and safety, and here was a nice, safe, slightly boring man who honestly cared for me. Let me tell you what a change that was from the men I've known before. And I really did love him back. So I convinced myself that he was right, that the Al Capones of the world took trips like anybody else and their money spent as well as anyone's. And if it was dirty money…well, is any money really clean?"

"You don't have to explain yourself to me, Lila."

"I know I don't. But I need to say it this once, just for myself, because I've never yet had anyone I could say it to. And now that I have, I don't feel like I'll ever need to say it again. I can move along." She reached over and laid a hand on mine. "And for that, Nate Ross, I thank you."

We finished our drinks mostly in silence, then she said she had to go, that work started early. I walked her out through the lobby and, out on the sidewalk, offered to drive her home. She thanked me but said she'd just take a cab, so I walked with her across to where they sat parked at the corner of Pershing Square.

At the cab stand, she suddenly turned and kissed me on the cheek. When she stood back, there was a sad smile on her face. "Thanks again," she said. "And good luck." She stepped into the cab and gave me a little wave, and I watched the cab drive away. I stood and tracked the cab's taillights going down Olive until they melted into the blur of the thousand other evening lights.

Chapter Six

B usiness had been good enough of late that I'd been able to take on a kind of apprentice a few months back. Mikey Galvin was a kid I'd nicked the year before pulling a kid-stuff caper. I'd treated him right, even introduced him to his hero—my old high school buddy, Duke Morrison, who was making cowboy movies under the moniker of John Wayne. It seemed to have made us lifelong pals.

Mikey was showing the makings of a decent gumshoe. With a little experience, he'd likely prove to be an ace at shadow work; being a gangly, goofy-looking kid with a pointy Adam's apple and kelp-green eyes made him look harmless and kind of simple-minded. Which was a laugh—the kid was as sharp as they make them and had all the guts, if not yet the skills, of a tough operator. But for the present, he had other talents that I found useful. He was studying criminal science, taking night classes in Burbank, and he had plans to go into the college program at Berkeley in the fall. He was a whiz at all the laboratory stuff, so I used him for most of my photo and fingerprint work. I could lift decent enough prints when I had to, but it was the kind of job better left to a specialist. I'd decided I'd be better off letting him dust the stuff from the Whitcanack case.

I'd stopped by his apartment to pick him up for the day's festivities and save him the car fare. While he was brushing his teeth and getting his things together, I passed the time talking to his father. Floyd Galvin was an okay guy when he wasn't soused, which meant you didn't often catch him in a friendly mood. He was more surly than usual this day.

"You get my boy hurt, I'm gonna twist your neck," he said between sips from a brimming coffee cup I was sure didn't hold more than an ounce of coffee. "I ain't just kiddin' you, neither."

"Mikey's almost twenty," I said. "He knows enough to watch out for himself."

"Yeah, well, I'm still his old man," he growled. "I ain't much, but I'm that."

"I don't put him on that kind of job anyway."

He gave me the fish eye. "You just remember what I said."

Mikey spared me any darker threats by appearing in the doorway, pulling his cheap fedora down over one eye. Dressed in a suit and tie, he looked a little less like a green kid.

"We're off to work, pop," he said. "See you for dinner."

"You watch yourself, Michael," Floyd called to our backs as we went out.

In the car, Mikey stared out the window as we made our way across town. I didn't think he'd overheard my conversation with his father, but I could see he was brooding over something. "What's on the mind this morning, Mikey?"

"Mike," he said without looking at me.

"Mike—sorry." Now that he'd put nearly two decades behind him, he insisted on giving up his kiddie handle. I kept forgetting.

"I've just been thinking," he said after a long pause, "If I'm gonna work in this trade, I'm gonna need a name."

"What do you mean a name?"

"You know, a nickname. Like 'Shadow' or 'Blackjack Mike.'"

"You're good with prints. We could call you 'Powder Boy.'"

"That's not funny."

"Or how about 'Mike-roscope'? Get it?"

"Knock it off."

"You've been reading too many pulps, kid. I've been doing this for years, and I don't have a nickname."

He looked at me with a grin. "Captain Queenan has a couple for you."

"I'll bet he does. And if I hear you using 'em I'll scrub your mouth out with soap."

"You ain't my pop, Nate."

"Don't be too sure that works in your favor, sonny boy."

We ate a quick breakfast at Gus's, my treat. Mikey's mother was dead, and his dad was out of work more often than in it, and what I paid the kid mostly went toward classes and books. So I tried to help out where I could without stepping on toes—the Galvins were a proud pair.

Afterward, we went upstairs to the office. I felt my daily pang when we passed the dentist's office—I missed dropping in to check for messages with Nina.

Mikey got right to work at his makeshift lab, a card table, and a desk lamp from the second-hand store. When we'd met, he was just a goofball kid. In a lot of ways, he still was, but put a fingerprint brush in his hand, and the boy was da Vinci. He could make clearer lifts than any copper or crime lab guy I'd ever known, and possessing a kid's keen eyesight, he could make accurate naked-eye comparisons nine times out of ten. On a job like that, Mikey was all pro, and he pulled his weight. Still, I didn't tell him yet what the case was. He was an excitable kid, and I didn't want him to get distracted.

To further avoid distraction, I decided to leave Mikey to his tasks while I took in a little fresh air and thought things over. It wasn't too hot outside yet, so I walked over to Barnsdall Park, just a couple blocks from my office. It was a hangout for a lot of artsy types who were fascinated with its acres of bucolic olive groves, colorful flower beds, and the big house that had belonged to the one-time owners of the property. To me, the thing looked like a cross between a Mayan temple and a mausoleum. But artists were late sleepers, so early as it was, I could avoid them and enjoy a quiet stroll among the trees. There were large fountains—one round and one square—on either side of the house, and I liked to sit on the grass at the edge of the big square one and just clear my head for a while.

I was in luck, and the park was almost empty. I made my way over to the fountain and found a nice dry patch of grass with a little shade. I sat and smoked a cigar, thinking of nothing in particular, and just for something to do watched a stray dog work his way down the winding path. A big, shaggy, reddish dog of uncertain breed, with ears that stuck up straight then folded over at the tips, and a broad head round as a bowling ball and nearly as large. He was built husky and solid, and if he'd been better fed, he'd have been a pretty formidable specimen. As it was, I'd put him at close to eighty pounds. He stopped a dozen feet short of a man sitting on a bench eating a sandwich out of a paper bag.

The bench sitter looked like the usual scratch house bum you'd see lazing around in any public park on any day that ends with *y*. He was a good-sized lug, with a red, scowling face that hadn't seen a razor all week. He alternated bites of the sandwich with slugs from a half-pint bottle he pulled from a side coat pocket. The dog sidled up to him, one eye on the sandwich, and settled his butt on the grass.

How a man treats animals tells me all I need to know about him, and I already didn't like this plug-ugly's looks, so I watched the two of them closely. He turned a fierce gaze on the dog.

"Go, on, get!" All that bought the guy was an expectant canine smile and a tentative thump of the tail. He lunged half off the bench. "Scram, I said!" The dog retreated a few feet, sat again, and whined. The guy sat back, sneered, and drained the last of his half-pint. Without warning, he slung the empty bottle at the dog, who yelped as it thunked off his skull with a hollow sound. I was about to get up and wander over to butt in on their conversation when the dog moved again, not away from the man, but closer. He laid his ears flat back, bared a set of wicked-looking teeth, and let out a low growl like the idling of a flathead V-8.

The rummy, instead of moving off like a sensible lad, laid his sandwich down and sprang off his bench and at the dog with surprising speed for his size. "Show me your teeth, will you, you mangy bastard?" Before I could get to my feet, he'd landed a vicious kick in the dog's ribs.

I pitched my cigar in the fountain and strolled over. The dog didn't yelp this time but backed out of kicking range and turned loose an even more threatening sound, like somebody had goosed the throttle on that V-8. I could read on tough boy's face that he was giving thought to launching another kick.

"Why don't you leave him alone." I didn't say it like a question. I didn't mean it as one.

It took the guy a moment. Rapid thinking wasn't a talent of his type. His head swiveled toward me, and when it sank in that I was speaking to him, he gave it an irritable shake. "What's that?"

"Leave him alone. Can't you see he's just hungry?"

The irritated look warped into a malicious leer. "Yeah? Well, why don't you mind your own damn business, bub, before I bounce somethin' offa *your* noggin?" In case that was too subtle, he held up a meaty fist.

The dog stopped growling and watched us both with keen interest. I ignored the guy's threat and picked up his half sandwich off the bench. I stepped over and squatted a few feet from the big red animal, holding the food out at arm's length. "Come on, boy. It's okay." He gave me a curious look, twitched his tail, and poked his nose toward the sandwich, ears forward and alert.

The sandwich's former owner just stood there in open-mouthed anger and disbelief. When his feeble brain finally clicked, he made a strangled sound of rage and roared, "Well, you son of a bitch!" I dropped the sandwich and stood as he charged at me. He was big, and he was quick, but like a lot of guys his size, he put too much power and too little precision in his punches. His looping roundhouse right sailed over my head without even taking my hat off as I ducked under and came up on his right. As he started to adjust, a little off balance from the missed blow, I gave him a sharp left to the side of the head. When he shook it off and pivoted to face me, I drove my right deep into his gut and gave it one more for good measure. I backed up and stepped aside just in time as he doubled over and shot the other half of the sandwich and most of his whiskey out onto the grass.

I was getting set for another round, but he held up a hand in surrender. Like all bullies do, he'd lost his starch once he saw he might not come out on top. He stumbled, coughing and wheezing, to the bench, plopped down, and started wiping his mouth on a sleeve. Meanwhile, I picked up the rest of the sandwich and fed it to the dog. He wagged his tail as he gobbled it down, then gave my hand a grateful lick. He stayed put and continued to wag when I walked over to the bench.

"I come to this park pretty often," I told the big boy, whose face was now about the color of the grass he'd just puked on. "Next time I do, you'd better have found someplace else to drink your lunch. You understand me?" I didn't really care, except that strays tend to stick to places they like, and I didn't want him coming back and taking the thumping I gave him out on the dog.

"Okay, cousin, okay," he croaked, nodding. He took a couple of deep, ragged breaths, then lumbered to his feet and shuffled off toward Vermont, only looking back at us once.

The dog just sat there and watched him go. Once he'd disappeared around the corner, the dog looked at me and started another tail-wagging jag. I crouched beside him and checked under his thick neck fur for a collar or tags. Nothing. I ruffled his ears, and when I started to pull my hand away, he gave it a bump with his head. I took that to mean he wanted some more, so I obliged, scratching between his ears and under his chin while he winked his eyes and gave me that blissful look you only ever see on a dog's face.

Finally, I stood up straight. "Well, old buddy, I've gotta get back to my day. I hope you'll be all right." I started off the way I'd come in, and when I'd gone a hundred feet or so across the lawn, I couldn't resist a look back. There was the big red hound, not six feet behind me.

"No, boy," I told him. "You need to stay here. Stay." I quickened my pace, and when I looked back, he was still trotting along right behind me. Vermont and Hollywood are both busy streets, and I didn't want him to get hit by a careless driver or mowed down by a streetcar trying to follow me across. I wasn't sure how to get that through to him—I'd been ten years old the last time I had a dog, and I didn't quite recall how to speak their language.

I noticed a piece of broken branch under a nearby olive tree and picked it up. It was about a foot long and twice as big around as my thumb. "Here," I said, holding it up. "You like sticks? Want to play fetch?" I tossed it a few yards off, and he watched it fall, gave me a questioning look, then trotted over and picked it up. He brought it back to me, and I threw it again, a little farther. He dutifully retrieved and returned it again. "Good boy," I said. Giving his head a final pat, I side-armed the stick as hard as I could, and this time it sailed a good twenty-five yards.

As he ran to pick it up, I hot-footed it toward Vermont and ducked behind a lamp pole. When I sneaked a peek, the dog was looking around him, bewildered, holding the stick in his mouth. Before I could move, he'd spotted me. He took a hesitant step in my direction, and I made one last "stay there" gesture with both hands, then turned and jogged across the street. I looked back from the other side to be sure he hadn't run after me. He was still watching me but hadn't moved. He stood looking at me for a few seconds, then dropped the stick and lay down on the grass.

I continued on my way back to the office. I felt like a heel pulling a trick like that on a trusting animal. But Hollywood was full of strays, some with four legs and some with two. And I'd learned a long time ago that much as you might like to, you couldn't save them all.

Chapter Seven

I figured Mikey could use more time, and I hadn't yet given any attention to this character Dubek. He definitely needed some looking into, especially since it was looking more and more like I was dealing with a murder. And whenever I needed the lowdown on any local players there was one place I could always count on getting it. I headed for the *Herald-Express* offices to see an old pal.

As I dropped into the chair next to Aggie Underwood's littered desk she thrust a sheet of paper at me. "What do you make of this?" It was a rectograph copy of a handwritten note. It read:

Cowards die many times before their deaths; the valiant never taste of death but once. Of all the wonders that I yet have heard it seems to me most strange that men should fear seeing that death, a necessary end, will come when it will come.

"It's from Shakespeare," I said. "*Julius Caesar.*"

"I *know*," she drawled, peering at me through her nose glasses. "I'm a little surprised that you do, though."

"Why's that?"

"Well, no offense, Nate, but you've never struck me as Joe College."

"Oh, I gave college a try. It wasn't for me." I handed back the paper. "But this I remember from high school—the senior class production."

"*You* were in the high school play? Did we have thespian ambitions?"

"We had a crush on Dorothy Albray. She was playing Calpurnia."

"I see. And were you the noble Caesar himself, or just a lowly spear carrier?"

"I was Volumnius, one of the guys Brutus asks to hold his sword so he can

51

fall on it."

"How apt."

I ignored her jibe. "I had a couple of lines."

"Were you any good?"

"The Barrymores have nothing to sweat."

"And did fair Calpurnia share that sentiment?"

"I guess so. She took up with one of the spear carriers. Last I heard, they're still married."

"Ah, well, the course of true love never did run smooth."

"That's *A Midsummer Night's Dream*, not *Julius Caesar.*"

"You *are* a dark horse, Nate."

"You have no idea." I handed back the note. "But what are you showing me this for?"

She shrugged. "It's from the suicide *du jour*. Poor guy shot himself with that note in his pocket."

"Jeez, another one? How many does that make this summer, anyway?"

"Who can keep up? Hell, there was probably at least one more while you were asking me that."

"And this guy wrote a Shakespeare quote as his goodbye note?"

She shrugged. "It's L.A. Nowadays, I guess you can't even kill yourself without giving it some artistic flourish." She pointed to the sheet in her typewriter. "I'm calling him the 'Boyle Heights Bard.'"

"Very catchy." Aggie loved giving snazzy nicknames to the cases she wrote about. It was becoming sort of a trademark.

"Anyway," she said, laying the suicide note aside, "I just thought it would interest you, since I hear you're working a suicide case of your own" She gave me a look. "Or *was* it a suicide?"

"Can't anything stay secret in this town?"

She laughed. "Not from me, it can't. And I'm betting that's why you're here. So what favor can I do for you today?"

"Fine. Can you dig into your files? Give me anything you've got on a bird named Charlie Dubek?"

"Dubek?" She snatched off her glasses. "Don't tell me that pit viper's mixed up in it."

"He came up. Why?"

"I can give you plenty on Charlie Dubek, and I don't need to look in the files to do it."

"So, who is he?"

"More like, *what is he*? Up front, he's a businessman. Runs a printing company, two blocks from City Hall. He has contracts with the city, the county, the state. Prints anything and everything the government needs, from business cards and letterhead to license forms, official documents, you name it. Go through your pockets and pull out your driver's license, your private investigator license, your gun permit—I'll guarantee you two out of three rolled off one of Dubek's presses."

"So, he's *connected*, is what you're telling me."

"You said it, kiddo. The word is he's got a wire into the mayor's office, if not the governor's. Anything political he needs done, or undone, he just makes a call. And there's talk of Mayor Bowron appointing him to the vacant seat on the Police Commission as part of his big cleanup campaign, so he's about to have even more juice." She gave me the dog eye. "What do you mean when you say he 'came up'? Don't go mum on me."

"He showed up while I was looking the dead guy's house over."

"Showed up in the flesh?"

"Two-hundred and fifty pounds of it. It seems the two of them had some sort of business connection."

"That doesn't narrow the field much. Dubek's got tentacles all over town."

"He seemed to think I should let the Whitcanack thing be."

She snorted. "And you, being Nate Ross, have declined to do so."

"It's the job. What can I say?"

"Tread lightly with this character. That's all I'll say."

"You know me, Ag."

"Yeah, I do. That's what worries me." She checked her wristwatch. "I'm about to head to Moran's for a bite of lunch. Join me?"

"Love to, but I've gotta go see a guy."

"What guy?"

I grinned. "Charlie Dubek."

She made an exasperated sound. "Why do I even bother?"

I didn't make Dubek for Whitcanack's killer, if anybody was. Dubek may hire a thing like that done, but he'd be far too savvy to soil his own shirt cuffs with it. Guys in his position farm out their kills, partly to protect themselves and partly to prove they have the juice. Even if he had done it, he'd have been a fool to go moping around Whitcanack's place afterward. He wouldn't have gone any closer to it than Grand Central Terminal.

I had no trouble finding Dubek Commercial Printing. It took up half a city block north of Temple and a baseball's throw from the Civic Center. I got as far as his personal secretary, only to be told that the big chief was out for the day. I made an appointment to see him for the following afternoon under a name that wasn't mine.

When I got back to my car, I noticed a blue convertible with a gray top parked several cars behind me. I was sure it was the same one that had followed me from Hockman's. I started down the sidewalk toward it. Glare from the windshield kept me from seeing who was inside, if anyone. Before I got close enough, I heard the car's gears mesh, and it jumped from the curb and made a sudden u-turn, leaving a chorus of screeching brakes, honking horns, and cursing drivers behind as it tore down Hill St. I was sure as it made the turn that I'd caught a flash of platinum blond hair through the driver's window. The midday traffic was so dense I didn't even attempt to follow, but I kept a close watch behind me all the way back to Hollywood.

After missing Dubek at his place, on a whim I drove over to the Hollywood branch of the public library. I was curious to speak to Alan Whitcanack apart from his sister. He hadn't shown much of his own mind in my office, and I wondered whether he really shared her suspicions or was just going along for the ride. Plus, I was picturing that blond head in the blue Chevy convertible.

When I asked for him at the front desk, the old bluestocking behind the counter grimaced at me like I was a schoolboy she'd caught reading Henry Miller. She informed me in a snappish tone that *Mister* Whitcanack had not

54

reported for work that day, nor had he called in. She said his absence was making things most inconvenient for the rest of the staff, which I took to mean her.

Having struck out twice in a row, I stopped for a bite of food, then headed on over to Westlake to give Mikey extra time to work and to deliver the promised report to my other client.

Alanna Whitcanack lived in an apartment within sight of Westlake Park. I'd wanted to talk to her first thing that morning, but she'd said her boss at the Hall of Records was a stickler and she couldn't afford to be late. Being a former county employee myself, I could sympathize. I'd also have preferred meeting with her at my office, or some neutral spot. Something about her—the two of them, actually—still struck a sour note with me.

She answered the door before I'd finished knocking and ushered me in. She was still dressed and made up for the workday, the Harlow wig in perfect order. The room she ushered me into was nicely done up in various shades of green—walls, carpet, and furniture all coordinated with obvious taste. But, like the girl herself, it was just a little off, and it took a few moments to figure out why. There was not a personal touch to be seen. No family photos or knickknacks, no vacation souvenirs, not so much as a half-read book lying open and face down on the sofa. Nothing to give a read on the person who lived there. It had the sterile, stagey feel of a model apartment, arranged to appear lived in but containing no actual life.

At her invitation, I perched on one of a pair of matching dark green armchairs while she brought in coffee in china cups on a little silver tray. The green vine patterns on the cup fit with everything else in the room.

"Would you like cream or sugar?" she asked as she handed me my cup. "I should have asked. I have some, but I don't use it myself."

"No, just like this is fine, thanks." *Black and bitter, like my soul*, I used to joke with Peggy. It always made her laugh. But I suspected Alanna didn't have my ex-wife's sense of humor, if she had any at all.

"Do you know where I could find your brother today?" I asked as Alanna started to settle into my chair's twin.

She paused midway and gave me a worried look. "At work, I'd assume. Why do you ask?"

"I stopped by the library earlier, and he wasn't there. They said he didn't show for work or even call in today."

She sat, frowned. "Well, that's odd. He likes to take time off and drive up the coast occasionally, but it's not like him not to call work if he wants a day off."

"Does Alan drive a convertible by any chance?"

She looked at me with curiosity. "He does. A beautiful blue Chevrolet, gray top. He just bought it not long ago. Why?"

"I'm jealous. Always wanted a convertible myself."

She smiled. "They're great fun until it rains. The tops always leak. But why were you looking for Alan?" The question sounded a little urgent.

"Just to get his take on things. He didn't say much the other day, but it's always helpful to talk to anyone who knew the deceased. Everybody's got their own knowledge of them, their own experience, a different point of view. You can never tell what information might turn out to be important."

"Yes, I suppose that's true. Speaking of which, you have some information to share?"

"I do." I sipped my coffee to buy a moment for my thoughts to get back on track. Brewed extra strong, and she drank her own without anything to smooth it out. Somehow that wasn't a surprise.

I gave her a quick account of my activities so far. The talk with the detectives, what I'd found—or not found—at her father's house. She seemed overly concerned when I repeated that I hadn't found fingerprints in the car. Detective stories tended to give people the impression that prints always make the case. She acted more at ease when I told her about the whiskey bottle.

I'd decided not to tell her everything—not yet, anyway. I wasn't sure how I could pass on all that Hockman had told me without tipping his mitt. And I wasn't going to mention that Alan had maybe been following me. I wasn't sure what to make of it, and I wanted to know the twins—especially him— better before I gave up too much.

56

"Now," I said, "if I can ask *you* for a little information, what can you tell me about Charlie Dubek?"

Her green eyes flickered at the name. "Charlie Dubek? He did business with my father—with his agency, that is. Why?"

"He showed up at your father's house while I was there. Had a key—says that he often looked after the place if your father was away."

I could see this bothered her, though she tried to hide it. "I wasn't aware of that," was all she said.

"Do you know Dubek personally?"

"I wouldn't say so, really. I've met him."

"What sort of guy is he?"

"I really couldn't tell you. As I say, we're barely acquainted. You don't—you don't think he had something to do with...."

"It's too early to think along those lines," I said. "Miles to go first." I sipped more coffee and watched her. I had the feeling she could say a lot more about Dubek, but doubted that she was going to.

"Anyway," I said, "I'd still like to talk to Alan. If he's gone for a long drive, when do you think he'll be home?"

"I couldn't say. Frankly, I'd rather you leave him out of things. He's a very sensitive person, so easily upset."

"But I assume he's as interested in finding out the truth as you are. Wouldn't he be eager to help?"

"Of course. But you may have...Alan is...an unusual person."

That much I'd already caught, but I asked anyway. "Unusual, how?"

She shifted uncomfortably, took her time futzing with her coffee without actually drinking any. Finally, she set the cup and saucer aside and took a long, slow breath.

"There was an accident," she said. "When we were six years old. We were outside, playing hide-and-seek with some of the neighborhood children. Our next-door neighbor was away. There was an icebox on his back porch—one of those old-fashioned oak things with the heavy brass hardware. Alan hid inside it, and somehow the door became latched, and he couldn't get out."

She stood up and paced a little. "It was hours before anyone found him, and there wasn't much air. They were able to revive him, but there was some permanent damage done, and he…." She sat again, staring at nothing, her eyes filling up. She started to speak but let out an explosive sob instead. I offered her a handkerchief.

"Thank you." She mopped at her eyes and crumpled the hanky in her fist. "He's ordinary in most ways," she said. "People get the wrong impression—he's actually quite intelligent. But ever since then, he's had occasional seizures, blackout spells. Not nearly as often now as he used to, but…." She blew her nose loudly. "He's been able to live on his own, drive, hold a job. But he'll always need someone to look out for him. Do you understand?"

"I think I do. A terrible thing," I added, not knowing what else to say. "How did your parents handle it?"

"Each of them in their own way. Mother had always doted on Alan. Afterward she was overly protective. But Father…" She looked away. "Father simply withdrew from him. Image was always very important to our father, you see, and having a son like Alan became a personal embarrassment to him, a secret shame. It caused a great deal of tension between my parents."

"And what about Alan?"

"Poor Alan didn't understand—couldn't, I suppose—why his own father shunned him. Mother tried to make up for it until the day she died." She leaned forward and spread her hands. "After that, it fell to me. I'm not sure how much Alan and father have even spoken since then."

"So it's fair to say there wasn't much affection between them either way?"

"I suppose not." Her eyes widened. "Surely you're not suggesting that Alan—"

"I'm not suggesting anything at all. Like I said, it's too early for that."

"What are you planning to ask him?"

"I'd rather keep that between me and him. And don't read anything into that. Anyway, I'm not sure, to be honest, until I know a little more."

Her voice got frosty. "I was under the impression I was paying you for answers."

"You're paying me for *one* answer. To the big question. And you need to let me go about finding it in my own way. Until I do, all the rest is just details."

"I suppose you're right." Her voice thawed a degree or two. "Just please be patient with Alan and try not to overwhelm him."

"I'm not going to give him the third degree, if that's what's worrying you. No blackjacks or rubber hoses. Like I said, I mainly want to know if there's anything he might know, or have seen, or heard that could help get you that answer."

She sat back and thought it over and seemed to relax. "Very well, Mr. Ross," she said at last. "I don't particularly like it, but if it eases your suspicious mind, I'll go along with it. For now. But please do keep me informed."

"I will," I said. "And call me Nate." I downed the last of my coffee, stood, and stepped to the door. With a hand on the knob, I turned and gave her what I hoped was a reassuring smile.

"And don't forget, Alanna," I said. "My suspicious mind is why you hired me."

After talking to Alanna, I was that much more determined to talk to her brother, if for no other purpose than to find out if he'd been shadowing me and, if he had, why. Plus, her talk about blackouts worried me a little. For the moment, though, I went back to the office to see how Mikey was making out with the fingerprints. When I walked in, he was leaning low over the table, squinting through a jeweler's loupe at a white fingerprint card. There were a few others beside it. He said hello but didn't look up or say anything more. I dropped in behind my desk and sat waiting while he examined first one card then another, and another.

"Okay," he said after a while, pulling his gloves off and laying them aside. He picked up two of the oblong cards and brought them over. He laid them side by side in front of me, and I stared down at the prints he'd taken from the bottle and beer can. He'd dusted the items with fine black print powder, then lifted the prints off with clear tape and affixed them to the cards. The result was the cleanest prints I'd ever seen.

"Sorry," he said as he brushed away a stray bit of powder that had stuck to the back of one of the cards and smudged my desktop. The ultra-fine powder

59

was like beach sand—it tended to get on and in everything. He pointed with a pencil to the card on the left. "This one has the prints from the can."

"So, Hockman's," I said.

He gave me a look. "Okay. And these," he said, pointing to the other card, "came off the bottle. Solid match, I'd say—both from the same person."

"You're sure of that?"

He looked hurt. "I double-checked it. You want me to show you all the comparison points?"

"No, sorry, I trust your call. So, anything else?"

He fetched another card from his table. "These are from the bottle, too. Without a full set of your guy Hockman's prints, it's hard to say for sure, but I'd guess a different person."

"How come?"

"Smaller hand. And the first ones are where you'd expect 'em to be if he was just holding the bottle or drinking from it, but these others...." He pulled open my bottom desk drawer and took out the bourbon bottle that rested there. How he knew it was in there, I didn't ask, but I made a mental note to mark the level. He turned the bottle over and picked up a pencil. "They were around the bottom, along here." He ran the pencil around the rim of the bottle's base. "But some of 'em," he said, tapping the pencil on the flat center of the bottle's bottom, "Were in here. Kind of screwy."

I thought about it. "If somebody was holding it upside down, gripping it by the bottom...."

"Why would they?"

"Maybe to pour down somebody else's throat" I was talking to myself more than to Mikey. "Somebody already lushed up that they wanted to get passed-out drunk so they could shut him up in a garage with the car running."

Mikey's eyes widened. "Murder? Jeez, Nate, you didn't tell me we were working a murder!"

"*We* aren't. You're doing some print work, period. Your old man would come after me with a hatchet if I brought you in on something like that. Besides, I can't say for sure yet that it *is* a murder."

"Well, who are you thinkin' these other prints belong to, the dead guy? Or is Hockman the dead guy? Or is he the killer?"

I knew I should have kept him in the dark. I told him just enough of the case so far to satisfy his curiosity. I told him what Doc Reese had said about Whitcanack's lack of fingerprints—I figured that would grab him, and it did. He snatched up a notebook and took it all down, saying he'd never heard of such a thing but was going to read up on it. Knowing the kid, by next week, he'd be an expert.

"So what do we—" He caught my look. "What do *you* do next?"

"Well, I have a little idea who I need to look at. First, I'm going to go talk to him. And if he's not home, I guess I'll go in and collect us some more prints."

"Let me do it." I started to shut that idea down, but he cut me off. "It's important, right? A murder case? And no offense, but you know I can do better lifts than you can."

"*No offense.* Why do people always say that just before they stick the knife in?"

"Come on, Nate. I can help. You've already let me shadow somebody. Twice."

"A girl boosting lipstick from Bullock's and an old man putting dog shit in his neighbor's mailbox. This is different."

"I'll do whatever you tell me to. And I won't get in the way, I promise."

I sat and gathered my thoughts for a bit while Mikey tinkered and made some notes. Watching him work, I decided maybe it *was* time to get the kid out of the office, under close supervision, and see what he was made of. Anyway, I knew if I didn't, he'd bitch about it for weeks.

Chapter Eight

Someday, some novelist or Black Mask writer will decide to skip all the hooptedoodle and pen a story about what a private investigator's day is really like. And nobody will read it. A few hardier souls may try, but they'll be snoozing before the third paragraph. If we got into as many fistfights, car chases, and shootouts as the pulps would have people believe, a p.i.'s lifespan would be about the same as a housefly's. At best, he'd end up eating all his meals through a tube. This was one of the lessons I was hoping to teach Mikey. Meanwhile, I left him sitting in the car while I went inside. He wasn't old enough yet to be in such places, and it being a bar, I was more than a little concerned we might run into his old man.

The Buscadero was an oddity on the streets of Hollywood, quite a feat in a town that had already pretty much cornered the oddity market. It was the new haunt of the anonymous movie cowboys who hadn't made a name for themselves and likely never would, even if they cared to. Day players, stuntmen, horse wranglers, and the like. For them, the usual Hollywood hangouts had no appeal, and the Hackamore Club, which had catered exclusively to their crowd, had been closed for nearly a year. My pal, Dusty Vanner, a member of this same frontier fraternity, had tucked away the better part of what he earned riding, roping, and twirling his oversized mustache for the cameras and put it into establishing a new oasis for thirsty Tinseltown cowpunchers. Dusty's buddy, Gerald Barnes, another celluloid cowpoke who, for reasons known only to God and himself, preferred to be addressed as *Pooter*, was his partner in the enterprise. I'd never asked, but I suspected that Pooter, having come from a wealthy Texas oil family, had financed the bulk of the venture.

I stepped into the cool interior and stood for a moment to let my eyes adjust from the white-hot sunshine outside to the bar's dim interior. Although it had been open only three months, the place had already taken on the comfortable, worn-in look and feel of a tavern that had been around as long as the town, if not longer. Nobody would have guessed that a mere six months before, it had been a Chinese restaurant. The boys had expended no little effort in purging the place of the pungent scents of peanut oil, soy sauce, and cooked cabbage.

The Buscadero wasn't nearly as spacious as the Hackamore, but it had the same sense of genuine old West blended with Hollywood hokum. Since it wasn't large enough to host live music, the boys had installed a Seeburg Symphonola, a massive thing that looked like an oversized floor radio but housed a phonograph inside its burlwood cabinet. At the drop of a coin, patrons could listen to the likes of Jimmie Rodgers, Patsy Montana, Sons of the Pioneers, or Gene Autry. The cowboys who drifted in and out kept the machine running constantly, as much for the novelty of the thing as for the music.

It wasn't running at the moment. The bar seemed deserted—a sign, no doubt, that its usual occupants were all out capering on movie sets. My pupils were still dilating when I heard a hearty "Howdy, Nate!" and the sound of boots clomping my way through a carpet of crushed peanut shells. My hand was seized and wrung in a tight knob-knuckled grip.

"Pooter there, pard!" It was Pooter's customary greeting to everyone, and he never failed to follow it with a belly laugh and a back slap hard enough to loosen molars.

"Hiya, Pooter," I managed to say when I'd gotten some of my breath back.

Pooter wasn't a big guy. He was only average height, no taller than Dusty, and had the same lean horseman's build. But he had the thickest forearms I'd ever seen on a man of any size, and the muscles on them were like ironwood. He looked nothing at all like the heir to a Texas oil fortune, and he acted nothing like the typical millionaire, at least not the ones they grew in Hollywood. In Dusty's words, Pooter was "as plain as homemade soap."

"Come on over, take a load off. Let me pour you a cool one." Pooter led me to the bar and, before I could protest, slid a frosted mug in front of me. I had to admit that as hot as the day was, the icy beer was a welcome treat. Pooter pushed his big hat back. "You're lookin' for Dusty, I expect."

I came up for air just long enough to nod. "If he's around," then dove back in as Pooter stomped over to a pair of swinging saloon doors behind the far end of the bar.

"Dusty!" he bellowed over the doors. "Get on out here; there's trouble in the house!" He came back down the bar and gave me a sly wink. Seconds later, the twin doors parted with a crash, and Dusty plowed through, his big stag-handled frontier Colt in his hand and the devil in his eye. The steely gaze swept the barroom and lit on me. He relaxed, shook his head, and stuck the hogleg in his belt. He ambled over with a barely visible grin showing under his huge handlebar mustache.

"God Almighty, Pooter. I thought we were being robbed or somethin'."

Pooter scoffed. "Now, why the hell would I bother yellin' for you if we was?" His hand came up from under the bar and laid an evil-looking shotgun, its twin barrels and stock both lopped off short, on the bar with a thunk.

"You see the sort of horseshit I put up with, Nate?" Dusty said as he offered a handshake, only slightly less painful than Pooter's. "What brings you around?"

I set my empty mug down and wiped foam off my lip. "I could use a hand, if you can get away for a while."

"Right now, you mean?"

I glanced around the empty bar. "If you're not too busy, yeah."

He looked over at Pooter. "Can you finish up that inventory in back? I reckon you owe me, anyhow, for scarin' about ten years off my life."

"So you're only gonna live to be a hundred and twelve, you ornery old bastard. Go on and have your fun. I can manage the *hacienda*."

I'd given Dusty a rundown of the case as we drove over to Alan Whitcanack's apartment. It wasn't far—a corner building on a quiet little street south of Santa Monica Boulevard, just across Gower from the cemetery. I left Mikey with strict instructions to wait in the car. If Alan was home, we wouldn't need Mikey, and I didn't want to spook the guy by bringing in the whole gang. Even if Alan wasn't home, there was always the chance that he or somebody else would walk in while we were searching, or a nosy neighbor would ring up the cops. So I'd planned for Dusty and me to get in, do our bit, and if everything was still jake, bring Mikey up to do his while Dusty and I stood lookout.

The apartment was only on the second floor, so Dusty and I took the stairs up, and I rapped on the door. If Alan was in, I wasn't sure how I'd explain the cowboy I'd brought with me, ten-gallon hat—which Dusty went nowhere without—and all. But I had the feeling I might need the help. Dusty had been a deputy marshal in his younger days, so he could be a handy guy to have along.

I knocked three times more. No Alan. For a guy who grew up on the prairie, Dusty was an ace with a pick—another reason I'd brought him. He made kid stuff of the lock.

He let us into an empty studio made up of only a small bathroom, a kitchenette, and a pull-down bed. An easy place for a search, and since there were two of us, we'd probably be out inside fifteen minutes.

We both slipped on gloves, and I started with the bathroom, where I least expected to find anything interesting. It held just the usual: shaving stuff, a couple of prescription bottles—nothing I could pronounce—in the cabinet, a hairbrush, tooth powder, and toothbrush. The toothbrush and the towel hanging on a hook next to the shower were dry. That bothered me a little.

The kitchenette was a bust. Both the refrigerator and cupboards were spotless and all but empty. It looked as if Alan ate most of his meals out. The main room boasted the same basic trappings you'd find in any furnished place, cheap and ugly but serviceable. The closet held a couple of suits, including the tweed job he'd been wearing when he visited my office. Also a few shirts, a spare pair of what I'd have guessed were his grandfather's shoes if I hadn't seen him wearing them, and an overcoat.

Dusty pulled down the bed. It was so neatly made I didn't like to disturb it for fear we'd never get it back into the same order. I settled for feeling around over the covers and under the pillows. Nothing. I lifted a corner of the mattress and looked underneath. Still nothing. I was about to call it quits and go for Mikey when something tickled at the back of my brain, and I went back to the closet.

The overcoat was a heavy number, black Melton wool, with the kind of big side pockets that have slits through on the inside so you can get to your pants pockets. I gave the coat a frisk and felt a heavy something in one of those pockets. I pulled out a book. Blue cloth-bound, with ornate stamped designs, one of those gaudy things they used to print in the last century. The fancy gold leaf script title read, *Songs and Hymns for Public Worship*. A bookplate inside the front cover said the book belonged to Althea Whitcanack. I flipped through the pages and found that they skipped from 216 to 219. Page 217/218 had been neatly stripped out.

"Ring-a-ding-ding," I said to Dusty.

After we finished, we went back downstairs, and I gave Mikey the high sign. He met us in the vestibule carrying his print kit in a big black satchel like a doctor's bag. Dusty took up a post in a little reading nook at the bottom of the stairs. I took Mikey up and ushered him in, pointing out the spots I wanted dusted. I reminded him he couldn't leave any powder residue or other traces behind—the trickiest part—and left him to his work. I took a chair in a similar nook at the top of the stairway, where I had a view of both the elevator and Alan's door. If anybody approached it, they'd have to pass by me. If anyone came up the stairway, we'd arranged that Dusty would cough loudly to let me know. I'd left him the photo of the twins; if it was Alan, he'd follow him up the stairs.

I lit a smoke and settled back with a copy of *Field & Stream* I picked up off the little side table. The library was limited: it was either that or *The Ladies' Home Journal*. I had no interest in knowing how to dress a deer or tie a hare's ear fly but had even less in learning how to grow hollyhocks or the best way to give my crystal stemware that spot-free shine.

After half an hour, I started to get restless. Mikey usually made short work of print jobs, but this was the first time he was doing one outside the classroom or my office, and his first go at breaking a law or two in the process. And since he'd had to wheedle me to let him do it at all, he knew that if he made a hash of things, it would be the last time. So I knew the kid was nervous.

After another ten minutes went by, I was getting the fidgets. I'd run out of cigarettes by then, which didn't help. I was just about to go tap on the door and tell Mikey chop-chop when the door across from Alan's opened. An old woman stepped out, a large purse in one hand and a mesh shopping bag in the crook of her other arm. She gave me a curious glance, and I touched my hat brim— just a polite, harmless, half-handsome guy catching up on his fishing lures. She smiled and nodded, then turned to lock her door. Just then, Alan's door opened, and Mikey stepped through, satchel in hand.

The old lady started and turned, and their eyes locked. Without skipping a beat, Mikey tipped his hat and gave her a five-dollar smile, then turned and called back through the doorway, "Thanks again, Mr. Whitcanack. I'll be back to deliver your order on Monday. And remember—we promise you'll be happy or your money back!" With that, he shut the door, sauntered past me, and went down the stairs, whistling. Damned if the kid wouldn't make a gumshoe yet.

We all piled into my car. Dusty took the back seat and pulled his hat down low for his customary snooze. I could hear muffled snores through the bushy mustache before we'd even left the curb.

"Sorry, Nate," Mikey said as I swung a u-turn. "Cleaning up took longer than I thought. You know how that powder is. And I tried all the places you asked for, and a couple you didn't, but the guy must be some kind of clean fanatic, washin' everything down regular. I couldn't find hardly any prints."

I was thinking I'd made a mistake, letting the kid try too much too soon. But if there was one thing he was tops at, it was print work. Maybe he was right. I could see Alan as the type who'd nurse a phobia about germs, or dust, or both.

"So what *did* you get?" I asked him as I pointed the Ford east on Santa Monica.

"Got a partial palm print on a chair back. One print off a knob on the radio, couple off sink handles in the bathroom, two or three off the inside of the front door. That's it."

"Nothing from the closet, the shoes?" He shook his head. "Bathtub? Medicine chest?"

"Zip." He shrugged. "Sorry. Maybe if I had more time to look—"

"Skip it," I said. "It's okay. We'll see what we can do with what you got. I just hope it's enough."

"I'm not trying to be a wise-ass, Nate," he said, "but why don't you just see if this guy's got a print card on file, get a copy of that?"

"Easier said than done, kid. The cops don't pass those out like Halloween candy."

"Maybe I could give it a try."

I gave him a look. "And just how the hell would you manage that?"

He shot me a grin. "I know a guy."

"Who?"

He just grinned and looked out the window. I didn't always tell him everything, especially when it came to my stoolies and sources, so I figured he was enjoying playing the same game on me for once. Fine, I thought, let the cocky little bastard try his luck. It'd be a good lesson to him on how the cops in our fair city looked on guys in my trade. And if he thought tossing *my* name around was going to buy him anything, he had a tough surprise in store.

To change the subject, I dug in my side coat pocket and took out the hymnal, wrapped in my handkerchief.

"Any chance you can get prints off this? Off the pages?"

He took the book, careful not to touch anything but the handkerchief. He looked it over, flashed that annoying, cocksure grin again.

"Duck soup, boss."

We dropped Dusty back at the Buscadero and drove back to the office. I pulled into the little gravel lot next to my building, and before I could set the emergency brake, Mikey said, "Hey, I think you have a visitor."

I looked toward the entrance to the stairway, and there, sitting like he was waiting for something, or someone, was the big red dog from the park. His ears and tail perked up as he looked our way.

"Oh, shit."

Mikey looked at me. "What's wrong, you don't like dogs?"

"I like them fine." I told him about seeing the dog in the park, maybe skipping a detail or two.

"What's his name?"

"How the hell would I know? I just told you, he's a stray." We got out of the car and walked toward the entrance. The dog ran to meet us halfway, tail whipping. Mikey intercepted him and, setting his bag down, took the dog's head in both hands.

"Hiya, boy. Good boy!" He looked up at me and grinned. "Looks like you got yourself a new pal."

"Oh no. I don't think so."

"Come on, Nate. What are you gonna do, leave the poor guy out here? He'll get run over, or the dogcatcher will get him. You know what happens to dogs at the pound if nobody claims 'em."

I did, and I'd also seen what the conditions were like there. I'd helped ship off a fair number of crooks to state prison, but I wasn't hard-hearted enough that I'd send even the worst of them to the dog pound.

"Why don't you take him home with *you*?" I asked.

"I wish I could. But our building don't allow pets, and Pop would never go for it even if they did."

"Well, I can't keep a dog."

"Why not? You live by yourself. He'd be good company. And he'd be a good watchdog, I'll bet. Look how big he is."

While Mikey was talking, the dog turned his attention to me, his tail still beating the breeze. He sat down in front of me and looked up into my face with a big, goofy dog smile, his tongue hanging to one side. As though he could lay it on any thicker, he raised a paw and raked it at my leg.

"See, he likes you," Mikey said. "Come on, Nate, just give it a try. What can it hurt?"

It's hard to ignore a kid's enthusiasm, even when that kid's about as tall as you are. I looked at Mikey. "You're not going to shut up about this, are you?" He just gave me his irritating smile in return. "Look," I said at last, "I'll hold on to him until we can find him a home, but that's it. I'm sure I can find someone to take him in."

"Okay!" Mikey said. "I'll help out. I'll feed him and take him for walks, and I'll watch him when you need me to."

"You bet your ass you will." I stroked the dog's big round head. "Come on, you. Let's see if we can round you up a bowl of water."

Mikey laid the hymnal on his card table and spread it open to where page 218 ought to have been. He had me open the windows wide, probably more for the dog's benefit than mine. I'd borrowed an enameled spit bowl from Painless Van Holten next door and our guest had drunk it dry twice. He was now happily napping in the corner behind the desk on an old car blanket I carried in the trunk of my heap.

I called Alanna Whitcanack. She said she still hadn't heard anything from Alan. While I was on the phone, Mikey took an atomizer from his black bag and sprayed some stuff that smelled vaguely like rubbing alcohol over pages 217 and 220 of the book. After a few minutes, he carefully laid the still-open book on top of one of the corner filing cabinets. He told me not to disturb it and said he'd check on it the next day.

Meanwhile, he took off to look up the "guy" he said could get him a copy of Alan Whitcanack's print card. I offered to drive him, but he insisted on playing it cagey, said he'd take the streetcar. I didn't press him on it—may as well let the kid have his fun.

I was set to call it a day. I'd just grabbed up my hat when the bell doohickey on my door jingled again. I figured Mikey had forgotten something or changed his mind about the ride, but instead, a guy I'd never laid eyes on before came through the door. With exaggerated dignity, like he was expecting fanfare.

He was short and rail-thin, sixtyish, with sleek silver hair and dark eyebrows over humorless blue eyes separated by the straightest and narrowest nose I'd ever seen. His pince-nez glasses, thirty years out of date, made him look like Woodrow Wilson. I might have pegged him for one of those funeral home hustlers who try to shame you into Circassian walnut with wrought silver handles and tufted silk lining when a simple pine box does the job, except that he was dressed too well for that. His cashmere suit probably cost what I'd make in a year, and the knot in his deep burgundy tie looked like it'd been checked with a plumb line.

The dog came instantly awake and alert. He looked at me and, seeming to read that I wasn't worried, lay back down on his blanket. The man's blue eyes made a quick sweep of the room, pausing briefly at the dog, and I had the feeling those eyes had cataloged every detail, down to the dead fly on the windowsill. They landed on me at last, and the guy showed me a mouthful of too-white teeth. If it was supposed to be a smile, his eyes didn't know it.

"Mr. Ross, I presume? Nate Ross?"

I've never trusted a guy who shows you his gums when he smiles. "Guilty as charged," I said. I waited for him to close his lips over that shark-like grin. "What can I do for you, Mr...."

"Coombs," he said, holding out a shiny-nailed hand. "Martin Coombs." We shook, and he pointed to the dog. "Is he quite safe?"

"Tough to say. He's a new arrival, only here temporarily."

"I see." He gestured to a guest chair. "May I sit?"

"Sure." He did, and I took my own chair and set my hat on the corner of the desk. Coombs glanced at it.

"I hope I'm not delaying you."

"Nothing that won't keep. Now, what's on your mind today, Mr. Coombs?"

He produced a card from a filigreed case and laid it in front of me. I picked it up for a closer look. Linen texture, expensive paper. It declared in crisp black print that J. Martin Coombs, Esq. was an attorney with an office in the Spring Arcade Building. In my experience, lawyers showed up at my door for one of two reasons: to hire me or to sue me. I stuck the card in my pocket and gave him a questioning look, wondering which it would be this time.

He rested elbows on the chair arms and steepled his fingertips. "I have come here, Mr. Ross, at the behest of an individual whom I regretfully am not at liberty to name."

Lawsuit, then. "A client of yours?" I asked.

"Let us say a friend. I hasten to add that I am not calling on you in any official capacity but have agreed simply to act as an intermediary. An informal advisor, if you will."

"To advise the friend, or me?"

He bared the gums again. "You are perceptive, sir. An essential trait, I suppose, in your profession."

I wasn't in the mood for twenty questions, and his stuffy manner was starting to grate on me. "All right, I'll play along. What's your advice?"

"Merely this." He glanced at the mutt in the corner. "Let sleeping dogs lie, Mr. Ross."

"Uh-huh. Any sleeping dog in particular?"

"The police, I am told, have declared Cecil Whitcanack's unfortunate death a suicide. The coroner has corroborated their findings. Let the official ruling stand."

I was half contemplating throwing this jasper out on the seat of his expensive wool pants, or seeing if the dog knew how to sic. Although that might appease my pride, it wouldn't satisfy my curiosity, so I decided to hear him out first.

"Well, that's plain enough," I said. "And I'm guessing this 'advice' comes with some sort of additional caveat?"

"I beg your pardon?"

"An *or else* clause."

"Ah." More gums. "I am not privy to any specifics, but I have been given to understand that should you refuse to cease and desist, there would almost certainly be repercussions."

"Repercussions. To my business, or to my person?"

He spread his hands. "As I say, I am merely the messenger." With that, he stood, brushed imaginary dust from a sleeve of his coat. "But I strongly urge you to heed my counsel, Mr. Ross. Future messengers may be, ah, less agreeable."

He stepped to the door and, turning, said, "You know, Mr. Ross, I was acquainted with your father."

"I'm not a bit surprised."

He gave me one last look at his teeth. "Good day, sir."

I sat for a while and tried to puzzle it out. First Charlie Dubek and now this Coombs bird. I couldn't see any clear reason why either of them should kick at my poking around on Whitcanack, but it surely had somebody bothered. Coombs claimed it was "a friend." Dubek, or somebody else? Maybe Coombs and Dubek had a mutual friend. Or did they each have different reasons for warning me off? I didn't know enough about either of these characters to answer that question. Maybe somebody else could. I rang up Aggie Underwood.

"Ag," I said. "I've got another name to run past you."

"Be still my beating heart."

I fished out the card Coombs had given me. "What do you know about a lawyer named J. Martin Coombs?"

"J. Martin Coombs," she repeated. "I know him all right. We call him *Catacombs* 'cause he works strictly underground. Sewer level, to be precise. He's a fixer. And what he fixes tends to stay fixed."

"A fixer for who?"

"Gun for hire—for anybody who pays the freight. But he's worked for some heavyweight clients, including our honorable Mayor Bowron."

"How about for Charlie Dubek?"

"Wouldn't be surprised. Why—what's Coombs got to do with your suicide?"

"He dropped by here a little while ago to offer me some of the same advice Dubek did. 'Let sleeping dogs lie' was how he put it."

She whistled. "Dubek sent him?"

"He wouldn't say. Professional ethics, you know."

"You need to step careful with these guys. You're swimming among the sharks here."

I couldn't help chuckling at that, thinking about Coombs's toothy grin.

"I mean it, Nate. You follow me?"

"I follow you, Ag. Say," I said, looking for a change of subject, "you wouldn't want a dog, by any chance?"

"A dog? Is the sleuth racket so slow you're hiring out now to find homes for pets?"

"Forget I even asked."

I arranged for Benjy to watch the dog while I drove over to a pet shop on Western. I was going to need some food, and since I knew I'd have better luck pawning the mutt off if he didn't look like a mongrel stray, I thought I'd better pick up a collar. I came away with the collar, a sturdy leather leash, two glazed ceramic food/water dishes, a nail clipper, a bottle of shampoo, a hard rubber ball, a beef bone, and a box of dog biscuits, plus ten pounds of dry dog food which judging by the size of the monster I guessed would last about a day and a half.

The dog met me at the office door. No Benjy. I guess he didn't get that when I said 'keep an eye on,' I meant 'stay with.' I'd been hoping that it might give Benjy and the dog time to become pals, and maybe the kid would take him off my hands.

I took a quick look around, but there didn't seem to be anything amiss. At least It looked like I could trust the beast not to demolish the place if he was left alone for a while. "Good boy," I said, giving his ears a ruffling. He gave me no argument as I buckled the thick leather collar around his neck and attached the leash. I took him down the back stairs so he could answer nature's call, which he did—both of them—with gusto, in the little patch of dead grass behind the building. I loaded him into the car, and he sat, quiet and calm, on the passenger seat and watched out the windows while we drove home.

I lived in a small, rented bungalow in a middling court on the fringe of Silver Lake, not two miles from my office. It had a small yard in back, fenced all around. Not a lot of space, but enough for the dog to do his business, at least. And anyway, I reminded myself, this was a temporary arrangement.

When we went inside, the dog spent a few minutes sniffing and poking around the place while I poured myself a bourbon. When he'd finished his inspection tour, he came into the living room, sat at my feet, and looked at me as if to say, "What now, boss?" I finished my second bourbon, then fetched the other stuff from the car. In the kitchen, I set the bowls down next to the stove. I filled one with water and the other with the dry food. It looked like rabbit droppings and smelled nearly as bad, but the dog didn't seem to care. He gobbled it down in about four bites and went after the water, most of which he slopped over onto the linoleum. I watched from the doorway, and when he was finished, he turned to me with grateful eyes and came over to wipe his dripping muzzle on my pant leg.

"Hey, pal, I just had these cleaned!" I grabbed a dish towel and dabbed at my soggy leg, then mopped up the floor. He watched me, and I could swear I saw a mischievous twinkle in his eye, like he was enjoying a private joke. "I can see this is going to be nothing but fun," I grumbled.

I went to the closet to find an old blanket, and he followed at my heels. I didn't know it until I nearly fell over him when I turned around. I laid the blanket out in the least inconvenient corner of the living room, along with the rubber ball and the bone. He took the hint right off—he stretched his bulk out across the blanket, bumped the ball aside, and started gnawing on the bone. After a minute or so of that, he let out a weary sigh and rested his big cannonball head on his front paws.

"Tough day, huh, pal?" The big brown eyes rolled upward toward me. "Yeah, me, too." He yawned and closed his eyes. "Just don't get too comfortable here," I said. "This is strictly a short-term deal." He gave a soft snore in reply.

He continued to sleep while I made and ate a ham sandwich in the kitchen, then read the papers for an hour or so. I dozed off in my Morris chair, and when I woke it was almost nine-thirty. The dog was sleeping beside the chair. I took him out for a last break, then led him back to his blanket and went to bed.

Chapter Nine

I woke up to a strange buzzing sound. I wondered in my half-asleep haze if a bee had gotten into the house. When my head cleared a little and I sat up, I could tell the noise was coming from the foot of the bed. I leaned over to look, and there was the dog, curled up on his blanket with his bushy tail half covering his muzzle, snoring away. When I got out of bed, his eyes snapped open, and he jumped to his feet alert, eyes bright, and tail wagging.

I massaged my face and rubbed sleep out of my eyes. "Buddy, that's not how mornings work in this house." I staggered into the kitchen, the dog right behind me, and put coffee on the stove. He sat just outside the bathroom door while I showered and shaved and waited patiently while I half dressed, then he had his breakfast while I had my coffee.

Afterward, I finished dressing, then picked up his blanket and took it back to the spot in the living room. "Do you know 'stay'?" I made a palms-down gesture over the blanket. "Stay. This stays here, got it?" He just gave me a wide smile and smacked the floor with his tail. I had my doubts.

I took him out back, to the same yard he'd been in eight or nine hours before, but he acted as if it was terra incognita. He spent the better part of fifteen minutes sniffing at every single blade of grass, probing the manzanita hedge and the dahlias and marigolds in the little corner bed, chasing lizards, and trying without success to shinny up the birch tree after a squirrel that was taunting him. He paid no attention at all to my efforts to hurry the process along. Finally, when I was near the breaking point, he concluded it was time to get down to the business at hand. Only then did it dawn on me I

76

didn't own a shovel.

"Can we get going now?" I asked as he trotted back into the house, looking pretty proud of himself. I clipped his leash on and led him to the car, trying hard to think of someone, anyone, who might want a dog.

Thanks to my furry house guest, I was late getting to the office and already not in the best of moods. When I came down the corridor, my office door was standing open, and I could hear noises from inside. I eased up to the doorway and looked in. The place was a shambles. Drawers and cabinets hung open, bookcases were emptied, and the books in random heaps here and there on the floor, files and other papers were scattered like parade confetti. In the middle of it, Mikey sat on the floor stacking books and putting files in neat piles on the desk, trying to restore order.

"What the hell happened, Mikey?"

"Mike. I thought I'd come in early today, see what I could do with those other prints. I found the place like this."

"How'd they get in?"

"Picked the lock, I guess. The door was open when I got here." He stood up. "I know what you're gonna say. I know I locked it when I left."

"No, I'm sure you did, kid. Come here." I showed him the scratches on the lock plate where the door had been jimmied. "Wait," I said. "What do you mean when you left? You were gone before I went home."

"I came back last night to get the hymn book. Thought I'd lay it out at home, let it air out overnight."

I looked at the piles of books on the floor. "That may have been what somebody was looking for." I clapped him on the shoulder. "Hot damn, kid. Good job! You got it with you?"

"Safe and sound." He opened up his satchel with a proud grin and brought out the blue volume. "Came up with some nice, clear prints, too. Oh, and I also got this." He pulled out a sheet of paper and handed it over. It was a photostat of an L.A.P.D. fingerprint card, the type with a full set of prints taken when someone's booked for a crime. The name on it was Alan Franklin Whitcanack. Booked on May 11th, 1939, for public intoxication.

"Cops picked him up outside a bar on Ivar," Mikey said. "Trying to use his keys to open up someone else's car. Too stinko to walk home, so they booked him, tossed him in the tank for the night, and kicked him out in the morning.

"Well, I take it back, Mike. Damned if you're not earning your keep around here this week."

"I couldn't get a copy of the mugshot, but I did get a look at it. Blond hair—like a peroxide job almost, light-colored eyes, kind of scrawny-looking?" I took the twins' photo out of my pocket and showed him. "Yeah, that's the guy."

I surveyed the mess. "Once we're put back together here, I need you to get to work cross-checking those prints."

"Will do. I've got classes today, though, so I need to leave before lunch. But I'll take the stuff home and work on 'em after."

"Okay, I guess."

"Oh, before I forget," he said. "Bob Hockman called just before you got here, said to call him back. The number's on your blotter."

I rang the number, and Hockman picked up on the second ring. "I thought you slept days."

"Yeah, I do," he said. "I ain't been to bed yet."

"So what's keeping you up?"

"I got a little somethin' extra for you. An item I maybe forgot about the other day."

I guess I shouldn't have been surprised. "All right, I'm listening. Talk it up."

"No, this one you don't get for free, bud. I'm going to need me some gettin' out of town dough behind this."

"I'm not in the mood for games, Hockman."

"No games. This is the goods—two centuries worth. And a bargain at that, if you wanna break your case. Be at my crib in an hour, hand me two hundred U.S., and I'll spill the works." There was silence on the line. "You still there, Ross?"

"I'm here. I'm just thinking."

"Think on the way over."

"It'll take me more than an hour," I said. "I'll have to stop at the bank for the cash and they don't open until nine. And listen, if this is some kind of build-up, remember our deal."

"Yeah, yeah. Just hurry it up."

I left Mikey in charge of the dog and the office and was at the bank at nine sharp. There weren't many early customers, so I made it to Hockman's about nine-twenty.

I banged on the shabby screen door for five minutes, but no Hockman appeared. He said he'd been up all night, and it had been close to an hour and a half since then. The guy probably just dozed off in the meantime. The door was locked, so I pounded a little louder and called his name, but still got no answer.

I went around to the side of the house, where I had to wade through knee-high weeds to reach a couple of cracked and chipped concrete steps and another door. Through the window in the door, I could see that it led into the kitchen. By pressing my nose against the glass, I could see through the open kitchen doorway into the living room beyond.

There sat Hockman in the same battered armchair as before. *Sprawled* more than sat. I tried the door, but it, too, was locked. I was about to put knuckles to it, but something about the way Hockman was sitting bothered me. The one leg I could see stuck out at an odd angle. I gave the door a couple of loud taps anyway. When I didn't see him move, I picked up a billiard ball-sized rock from the weeds, smashed out the window, and reached in to twist the lock tab.

The sharp tang of gunpowder was faint, but still hung in the air. Hockman wasn't going to be getting his two hundred dollars. And I wouldn't be getting his story, whatever it was. Someone had put three slugs—.38s from the look of it—into the middle of him. He was slumped in the chair with eyes and mouth wide open and a look of utter bewilderment on his face.

I used my handkerchief to pick up his phone and call the cops, then went outside to smoke and wait.

Two patrol coppers showed up fifteen minutes later. After they'd spent another twenty minutes tromping around and messing up the scene for the detectives, Lockwood drove up with Queenan in the passenger seat.

Queenan shook his head as they came up the walk. "I oughta be back at the barn shuffling papers, but when I hear we got a fresh one and Nate Ross is the reporting party, I just know I'm in for one interesting ride."

"'Reporting party' is it this time. I didn't shoot this one."

"Blah—so *you* say." He winked at Lockwood.

"What really brings you out in the sunshine, Captain?" I'm sure you didn't come all this way just to bust my hump."

"Nah," he said around his cigar. "Been meaning to call you anyway, see how you're doing on the Whitcanack deal." He grinned at Lockwood. "You know, in case I need to make travelin' plans." If Lockwood got the joke, he didn't show it.

"I'm going to go see what we've got, Cap," he said. Queenan gave him a nod, and Lockwood said a quick, "How you doing, Ross?" as he moved around me. He went inside without waiting for an answer.

I wasn't sure how much I wanted to tell Queenan. So far, he'd been uncommonly, even suspiciously, helpful. But no copper likes being told, let alone having it proved, that he's wrong about a case.

"I'm still just plodding along, talking to everybody involved," I told him. It seemed like a safe enough answer.

"Uh-huh," Queenan said, flicking ash onto the dead lawn. "Which tells me a whole lotta nothin'."

I turned up my palms. "They call us *private* investigators for a reason."

"Uh-huh," he said again. He gestured toward the house. "But now we got us a bona fide murder of a party concerned in your case. And you playin' the cagey line tells me you figure I ain't gonna like how that case is goin', or *where* it's goin'. Try me—I might just surprise you."

"You already have. Normally you'd tell me to take the air the second I came around looking into a case you'd already put paid to. But you didn't."

"So," Queenan tried to blow a smoke ring. "Mister private *dee-tective*, don't that maybe make you think?"

I hadn't really taken the time to consider it until now. Something was obviously on Queenan's mind, but nothing with him ever came easy. He had to make you work for it.

"If I was to take a wild guess," I said at last, "I'd say you boys knew all along Whitcanack was no suicide, but you wrote it off as one anyway."

"Now, what would make me do a thing like that?"

"Well, so long as we're playing *what if*, I'd say—and no offense meant—that a captain's only about midway along in the department's pecking order. You've still got a boss, and he's got a boss, and so on, right on up to Chief Hohmann. Hell, even *he's* got a boss. And from what I read, he wasn't the mayor's first choice anyway, so he's gotta play nice with Bowron, at least so long as those stars on his collar are still shiny and new."

Lockwood stepped back out just then. Queenan burned a little more tobacco and winked at him again. "See, Billy, didn't I warn you this guy's sharper than he looks?"

Lockwood gave me a confused look. "You did that, Cap." He turned to me and, while he took careful notes, asked me to run down my actions from the time I'd arrived there until the first cops showed up. He saved the obvious question for last. "What brought you out here this morning, anyway?"

I wasn't ready to spill all the beans just yet. I told him only that Hockman had called me and said he had some more information about Whitcanack. I didn't mention that he'd hinted he could hand me the killer—for a price.

Lockwood's face told me he didn't buy my answer, but he took it down without saying so. A couple of lab guys showed up while we were talking, and with polite nods, they shouldered past us and went in, lugging their cameras, print kits, and other paraphernalia.

"Hey, Billy," Queenan said. "If you wanna go sheepdog them boys, I can keep tabs on Ross here. Don't worry. If he makes a break for it, I'll gladly shoot him."

Lockwood gave him a close look. "Sure thing, Cap," he said and went back into the house.

As soon as Lockwood was gone, Queenan picked up the conversation right where we'd left off. "So you're suggestin' a good old L.A. hush?"

"Like I said, if I was to guess."

Queenan chewed on that for a bit. "Well, I ain't gonna tell you you're right, and I ain't gonna say you're not. But if there was such a thing goin' on, why do you suppose that would be?"

And there it was. Queenan had been shut out of his own case and didn't know why he had, and both those things rankled.

"Search me, Cap," I told him. "But if it tells you anything, Charlie Dubek's involved somehow."

His eyes sparked. "Dubek?" He dropped his cigar butt in the dirt, ground it under a heel. "Involved how?"

"I don't know, and that's gospel. But he evidently had some sort of dealings with Whitcanack outside of their normal business connection. He showed up at Whitcanack's house while I was there. Had a key. I saw him looking for something."

"Lookin' for what?"

I shrugged. "No idea. But whatever it was, he didn't find it, and that didn't make him happy."

He mulled that over while he took his time trimming a fresh cigar. "What do you know about Charlie Dubek?" he asked at last.

"Only what I've heard. He's got government contracts out the keister, and he draws water in this town."

"He does *and how.*"

We could hear Lockwood's voice rising from inside the house. He was chewing somebody out. Queenan grinned. "I like that kid," he said. "And what he don't know they can't hold against him."

He motioned for me to follow. We walked to the curb, and he leaned on their car and lit his cigar.

"What's with the cloak-and-dagger all of a sudden?"

He closed one eye and pinned me with the other. "I never told you none of this, get me? We never had this talk."

"Haven't even seen you in days, Cap."

He nodded. "This asshole Dubek—we've had our eye on him for a while. Couldn't touch guys like him under Davis, and with the temp chief, who knew? I was hopin' things might be different with Hohmann at the helm."

"But?"

He cocked his big chin toward the house. "Lockwood had no more gotten to the Whitcanack place before he had a deputy chief breathin' down his neck *suggestin'*—and you know what that means coming from one of the high muckety-mucks—that he was clearly dealin' with a simple case of suicide. It didn't smell right to Lockwood, so he called me, and I talked to the deputy chief myself. I about got my ear torn off for my trouble."

"Which deputy chief was this?"

"Nix. I'm keepin' that in the family for now."

He chewed his cigar and looked at nothing for quite a while before he spoke again. His face had gotten red around the edges. "But I'm tellin' you, Ross, it burns me when some son of a bitch politico who don't amount to a wart on a copper's ass tells me how to run my cases."

"Are we still talking about the deputy chief.?"

He shook his head. "He was just the middleman. I know that much. What I don't know is why. But what I hear is, the mayor's all set to name Charlie Dubek to the police commission."

"Yeah, Aggie Underwood told me the same thing."

"I guess she'd know," he said with a smirk. "Her rag and the *Times* are both backin' the shitbird for the job. And I don't have to tell you what a sweet deal that would be for Dubek. A position like that, Bowron might as well be givin' him the plates to print his own *dinero*."

"So, you figure the mayor had you called off Whitcanack?"

"Makes sense, if Whitcanack was caperin' with Dubek. If it's a murder instead of a suicide, that could end up throwing some light on Dubek, maybe drag out a skeleton or two he'd like kept in the closet. That'd for sure scotch the appointment, and worse, it would leave Bowron with egg on his face."

He took a furious drag on his cigar. "If it was just my ass on the line, I'd have told the deputy chief to go piss up a rope, but I didn't want Lockwood to have to eat a turd."

"Getting mushy in your old age, Cap?"

He yanked the cigar out of his puss and glowered at me. "Kiss my ass." The look softened a little. "The kid's a good egg, got a wife, kids, his whole career ahead of him. And he's sharp and square. You know as well as me we could use more guys like that. Hell, he'll probably be chief himself someday."

"You said you've had your eye on Dubek. Eye on him for what?"

"His printing racket's right enough, as far as it goes. Nothin' but the usual kickbacks when public contracts are on the table. But under the table, Dubek's got other ventures."

"Such as?"

"The wise boys in town say he's the bird to see if you're a guy lookin' to do a fade-out. You need to go away for good— new name, new papers, new address, and so on—Dubek can provide. For a price, naturally."

"How's he work it?"

He shrugged. "We never got that far. With Davis in the big chair, we had to work it on the q.t. Since then, it's been wait and see how the wind blows. But it's not too hard to figure. The guy's a printer, so bogus documents would be a cinch. And your boy Whitcanack bein' a travel agent... If he was playin' in the sandbox with Dubek, it listens, don't it?"

"You said *ventures*. Is there more?"

"Just some rumors. That Dubek might also be playin' both ends against the middle."

"How's that?"

"Supposed to have kept a book. A record of all his crook clients, where they landed, names they're usin' now. Word is he's tappin' some of 'em to keep the hush on their whereabouts. They pay the guy to make them disappear, then he makes 'em keep payin' to stay disappeared."

I whistled. "That'd be pretty risky business."

"You ain't shittin'. Good way to end up pushin' up the poppies."

"Did a lawyer named Coombs ever come up in any of these rumors?"

"Marty Coombs?" He made a disgusted face. "Not that I heard, but there ain't much dirty dealing goes on around this burg that that shyster don't get his nickel out of. Why do you bring him up?"

I told him about the warnings I'd gotten from both Dubek and Coombs.

He shook his head. "Sounds like you're for sure shakin' the right trees."

Lockwood was coming out of the house and toward us, so Queenan didn't say anything more.

"The meat wagon's on the way, Cap," Lockwood said, "and the lab boys have about finished with photos and prints. I'm gonna get the blues started checking the neighborhood, see if we can turn up any evidence or witnesses."

"Okey-doke, Billy. You all through with Ross, here, or should I cuff him and stuff him?"

"No, I think that's enough for now." Lockwood looked at me. "If we need to follow up, I guess we know where to find you."

Chapter Ten

I showed up fifteen minutes early for my appointment with Charlie Dubek. The same secretary greeted me with the same bland courtesy, and after I'd cooled the dogs in the lobby for ten minutes, she waved me in. She ushered me down a long, stuffy hallway that, for all its mahogany paneling and deep carpet smelled of machine oil and printers' ink.

We stopped near the end at a double-wide door upholstered in burgundy leather with big brass buttons. With a little grunt of effort, she swung it open "Mr. Van Overschelde to see you, Mr. Dubek," she announced, then backed out and pulled the big door closed.

Dubek stood from behind a massive desk piled high and wide with printed ephemera of all sorts. His jacket was off, and his shirtsleeves rolled up over thick, hairy forearms that tapered like a pair of Indian clubs. Off to his side, near the windows, stood a guy in ink-spotted work clothes, a cap, and a denim apron. He was short but wide as he was tall and solid built, with carroty red hair and a face like a chimp.

Dubek started across the room with a big hand extended and a politician's smile but pulled up short when he clocked my face. "Hold on now," he said. He thought for a second or two. "Ross, wasn't it?" His eyebrows crowded each other, and the smile faded. "Say, what's the gag?" The little guy stood up straight and put a hand under his apron.

"You weren't in when I stopped by yesterday," I said. "And I wasn't sure you'd see me if I gave the secretary *my* name."

He chewed on that some. "Why the hell wouldn't I? I got nothing to hide." He looked at the small man. "S'okay, Eddie, you can get back to the presses."

Eddie gave me what he supposed was a hard look, then walked out. "Well, you're here now, anyhow," Dubek said. He waved a big paw at his guest chairs. "Sit, sit."

I did, and he lowered his own bulky body into the padded swivel chair behind the huge desk. He gave me a lopsided grin. "Gotta say, I'm glad you ain't really this Van-whosis. I wasn't lookin' forward to tryin' to repeat *that* name." He leaned in. "So, what brings you to me?"

"Cecil Whitcanack."

"Yeah. We talked about that already. Don't know what more I can tell you."

"I was hoping to find out a little more about your business. I've been hearing some things, but I'd always rather get them from the horse's mouth, so to speak."

"Lookit, guy." He leaned back until the chair crackled under his bulk like a string of ladyfingers. "I can guess what the boys downtown been feedin' you about me, and I'm tellin' you it's the bunk."

"So you're not a mover and shaker?"

"I dabble in politics, sure, but it's all in the daylight. I'm a law-and-order boy down to my shoestrings. Hell, I helped Gene Biscailuz get elected sheriff, twice."

He hadn't asked enough questions about me, or he'd know that wasn't the claim to sell me on his civic virtue. But I nodded as if it did. "Okay, so you're a right guy, public-spirited, honest as the day is long."

"You mockin' me, gumshoe?"

"Not a bit," I lied. "Just trying to line up my facts."

He gave me the dog eye. "Yeah, right. So what other *facts* can I help you line up?"

"Well, back to your business. I'd like to know more about your dealings with Whitcanack. And I don't mean business you did *for* him, I mean *with* him."

His eyes went stony. "I can see you decided not to take my advice."

"Neither time."

"You might end up regrettin' that."

"Buddy, I've got nothing but regrets. I'll throw it on the heap."

"Yeah, but I'm not sure you're getting' the picture here. See, I crook my finger, and you're a memory."

He tensed as I reached inside my jacket and relaxed when I brought out my cigarette case. I took my time lighting up. "Figure of speech, right?"

He didn't answer, just stared at me for a long while. He took a deep breath at last, rocked forward, and leaned his heavy forearms on the desk.

"Okay, pal. I can see you're a guy who won't be buffaloed, and that you ain't gonna let this thing go. I don't like that, but I respect it. So I'm gonna level with you, because I think you're a bright enough boy to see that if somebody did kill Whit it had nothin' to do with me. And then I'm trustin' you to keep my name out of it."

"And if I don't?"

"Let's keep it friendly for now. I think you will."

"All right, what does you leveling with me sound like?"

He smiled. "First of all, I doubt I'm givin' you anything the cops haven't already. But if they could prove any of it, or move on it if they did, I'd be in stir already." He grabbed a decanter of Scotch and two glasses from a tabouret stand beside his desk. "Snort?"

"Sure." He poured, and I tasted. Top-shelf stuff, of course.

He downed half of his in one throw and smacked his lips. "So ask what you wanna ask."

"Okay. You and Whitcanack were running a racket supplying crooks with fake papers, new identities, relocating them so they could disappear—escape the law, their enemies, whoever. Right so far?"

He winced. "I don't like that word 'crooks.' Not everybody that wants to start a new life is doin' it to stay ahead of the law."

"Fair enough. You help out *people* who want to disappear. For whatever reason."

He turned his glass on the desktop, nodded at it. "Correct."

"Who else is in this scheme besides you and Whitcanack?"

He grinned. "See, now that touches on things the cops may *not* know about. Pass."

"All right, then. I assume the phony papers get printed up here?"

The grin widened. "No comment."

So much for leveling. "What was Whit's part in all this?"

"He's—well, he *was*—the contact guy. Travel agency's a perfect front, see? Clients would go to him, spell out what they needed—passports, driver's licenses, diplomas, whatever. He'd hand all that off to me. And then he'd make their travel arrangements—train or plane tickets, lodging on the other end, all that sort of stuff."

"There's talk he was running his own game on the side," I said. "That he kept a book with clients' names, the new names they were using, where they were living, and was using that info to bleed them." Queenan had said it was Dubek's scheme, but I'd started to think maybe the book, if there really was one, was what Dubek had been looking for.

"Bullshit." He sat up straight. "How long you think a racket like ours would last if word got around that kind of grift was goin' on? A few of our clients are some pretty hard babies. You think they'd sit still for bein' blackmailed? Gone don't mean you ain't still got reach."

"So maybe that's exactly what happened to Whit. Somebody reached."

"Aw, you got squirrels in the attic if you believe that."

"Why not?"

He jabbed a thick thumb at his chest. "Because I'm still breathin'. And I'm still in town. Don't go thinkin' my mama's baby boy's so foolish or brave he wouldn't do a quick fade-out if guys like that were doggin' him. Trust me, that book ain't nothin' but some copper's fever dream."

"Maybe. But if it isn't, there's another little idea."

"Which is?"

"Maybe Whit's partner didn't take kindly to his playing his own hand. Or maybe he wanted the book all to himself."

He roared with laughter. "Oh, brother, I can see that fever's catchin'!" He mopped his eyes with a wrist and knocked back the rest of his Scotch. "Listen, Ross, 'cause I'm gonna say this plain, and I'll only say it this one time. I did not kill Whit. And I did not have him killed. I doubt you'll believe it, but I liked the guy. He was a good egg and a good partner. And whatever else I am, I'm loyal to my friends."

I finished my drink and set the glass down. "Let's say I buy all this," I said. "Since you and Whit were such good pals, why don't you tell me who *you* think killed him?"

"Look, the guy was still broken up over his wife. What I hear, his fiancée just gave him the toss. You've met his kids—the son's a little creep and Whit had some kind of falling out with the daughter. Fellow like that maybe starts thinkin' to himself, 'What's the point?'" He looked me in the eye. "I think the poor guy just decided he'd had enough."

If I believed nothing else he'd said, I believed that. At least that he believed it.

"Now," he said, looking at his watch, "I know I got a few other appointments today. People that left their *right* names." We stood, and he walked me to the door.

"I'm tellin' you the truth, Ross," he said. "Whit and me were friends. I'm a good friend to have. And a bitter enemy. You'll want to remember both them things."

"I'll remember."

Mikey was gone when I got back, and the dog, as usual, was asleep. I locked him in the office while I went down to Gus's for a quick lunch. Gus Karavolos, the boss himself, was in for a change. I took advantage of the rare appearance and asked him when I paid my check if he wanted a dog. All I got in reply was a rumbling laugh.

"You crazy in your head, Nate," he said. I could still hear him laughing when I was halfway across the little gravel parking lot.

When I went back upstairs, I saw Queenan and Lockwood leaning on the wall outside my office door. I hadn't seen them drive in. Lockwood elbowed Queenan, and the captain turned and eyeballed me through his cigar smoke haze.

"What's the matter, Cap?" I said. "You forget your jimmy?"

"Oh, I slipped the lock all right," he said. "We was plannin' to cool our heels inside 'til you got back. But that grizzly bear somebody's stuck in there had other ideas."

Maybe Mikey was right about the watchdog thing. I stifled a laugh. "Come on in, gents. I think we'll be safe enough." We went in, the cops close behind me with Queenan bringing up the rear. The dog rose to his feet and plastered his ears back against his skull. He peeled his lips back, and a rumbling growl started deep in his chest.

"Easy, boy," I said. "These guys are friendly, more or less." I laid a hand on the broad head, and the growl died off. He looked up at me, then eyed the two cops with suspicion. But when I sat, he relaxed and lowered himself back onto his blanket.

"Jesus, Ross," Queenan said, giving the dog an uneasy glance. "You startin' up a zoo or what?"

"It's a long story. He's a stray I'm looking after for now."

"Well, ain't you a big softie?"

Queenan took the guest chair closest to the door. He looked the dog over. "You know, this could maybe be a good sideline for you." He jerked a thumb back over his shoulder. "You could hang a sign out front— 'Ross's Home for Wayward Dogs. Bark twice for Nate.'" He grinned and looked over at Lockwood for approval. Lockwood gave it a courtesy laugh.

"So what brings you boys around?" I asked. "I'd have thought you'd seen enough of me for one day."

Queenan kept an eye on the dog as he talked. "Just wanted to let you know you left Hockman's too soon. You missed the best part of the show."

"How's that?"

"We found a gun in the hedges beside the house," Lockwood said. "A little .38 Iver Johnson top-break. Three out of five rounds in it spent."

"The gun that did it?"

He shrugged. "Too soon to know, but if I was a betting man.... Looked like the print boys pulled some decent latents off it. So we'll see what we see."

"Well, that's nice work, gentlemen. I hope it pans out. But you could have told me that much over the phone. You didn't have to come here and risk getting mauled. So I'm gonna guess there's more to this visit."

"A couple of things," Lockwood said. He looked at Queenan.

Queenan waved a hand. "Your case, Billy. Go ahead." He sat back and dropped a little ash on my semi-clean floor. Lockwood pulled out his notebook. It took him a second or two to find the page he wanted. "First of all, this guy Hockman. Turns out he matched a circular we had from Nevada. His true name was Chester Knox. Did five years at Carson City for armed robbery. Made parole last October, and they haven't seen him since."

He closed the book and studied me for several seconds. "From your reaction, I'm guessing you already knew this." I looked over at Queenan. He had a light in his eyes like he was laughing inside at a gag nobody but him understood.

"I knew he'd jumped parole," I admitted. "At least he told me he did. But I didn't know from where or for what, and he wouldn't give me his real name."

Nobody said anything. The two cops just looked at each other. To break the silence, I said, "Does it really matter? I'm a P.I., licensed in the state of California. What the hell do I owe the Nevada prison system?"

"There's that," Queenan said. "Tell you the truth, I don't give a damn either. We're not gettin' paid to clean up Nevada's problems. The thing I'm—we're—wonderin' is this: Did you maybe have this bird down for killin' Whitcanack?"

"Oh," I said. "*That's* what's on the mind. Well, I hate to disappoint you boys, but no, I had nothing like that on the guy. In fact, I've got some pretty clear evidence that it *wasn't* him."

I decided to level with them, to a point. I told them what Hockman had said to me on the phone earlier. I left out my first talk with him and the suspicions I had about Alan Whitcanack and his father. The guy was still technically a client, and I wasn't about to give him up unless I was dead-bang sure. But they both sat bolt upright when I laid out why I'd gone to Hockman's.

"Why the hell didn't you tell me this at the scene?" Lockwood asked.

"What's the difference? There's no guarantee he was shot because of what he was going to tell me. If he even *had* anything to tell, and I have my doubts about that."

"But it's a pretty damn good bet that's why he was clipped, don't you think?" Lockwood was getting a little heated, and the dog raised his head to give him a warning look. I reassured him with a pat, and he plumped back down with a token growl.

"Not necessarily," I told Lockwood. "Pretty sloppy work if it was. Think about it. If someone chilled Hockman—or Knox, I guess—to keep him from spilling on them, why the hell would they leave the gun behind?"

"Could be they didn't intend to. Maybe they dropped it."

"Bullshit. I know the hedges you're talking about. They're not in a path anybody would take if they were running away from the scene. Anyway, you said 'in the hedges.' You don't drop a gun into a hedge, you *put* it there."

He shook his head. "Either way, you should have told us."

"Well, you know it now. Is anything different?"

Lockwood slapped his notebook shut and turned away with an angry huff.

Queenan had just sat and watched us with that half-amused look on his face. He took out his wallet, pulled out a grubby dollar bill, and waved it at Lockwood. "Billy, be a pal and trot downstairs to that diner. Bring us back some coffee and a couple of sinkers, huh?"

Lockwood's eyes were still angry. He started to say something but checked himself. He stood up and took the bill. "Sure thing, Cap," he said in a flat voice. "Be back in a jiffy."

"No hurry."

When he'd gone out, Queenan looked at me. "The kid's right, and you can't tell me he ain't. You go holding out on a murder case, pal, you're paddlin' your boat right up shit creek."

"Yeah, I know, Cap, I know."

"I guess you had your reasons, or you thought you did."

"I was just trying to keep my case from getting muddled up in yours. And I'm still not convinced they're connected. If Hockman was a con, a fugitive, and a stick-up man, who knows what kind of enemies he's made along the way? Or friends, for that matter."

"Maybe. But you been in this game long enough to know how often a coincidence is a coincidence."

"I guess."

"Funny thing is, Lockwood likes you. After you came to see him, he told me you weren't the guy he was expecting. "He chuckled. "He said you struck

93

him as a 'quiet, unassuming guy.'"

"Well, I'm sure you set him straight."

"I tried to once I quit laughin'. I told him a hand grenade's quiet until some joker pulls the pin." He flicked more ash on the floor. "Look, I'll talk to him. He'll settle down. He just don't know you like I do, the lucky bastard." He chuckled again and pointed the soggy end of his cigar at me. "But this is *you* owing *me* one."

Footsteps came down the hall. As Lockwood shouldered through the door, juggling three paper cups with a greasy brown bag dangling from his fingertips, Queenan shifted gears.

"So tell me, what's your dog's name, anyhow?"

Lockwood passed a coffee to Queenan and set one down in front of me. He rolled the top down on the bag of donuts, placed it on the desk, and settled back into his chair.

"He's not my dog," I said. "It's just a temporary thing." I fished out a donut and burned my lip on the coffee.

Queenan and Lockwood each took a donut. Queenan started to bite in but stopped and turned to Lockwood. "You got my change?"

"I tipped the kid two bits."

"Blah." Queenan bit off a hunk of donut and talked around it as he waved the rest at me. "You still got to give the dog a name, Ross. How else you gonna call him when you want him? Tell him to quit lickin' his privates?"

"I'm not going to have him long enough to worry about it. Say, I don't suppose either one of you—"

"No dice, pal," Queenan stuffed more donut into his face. "Me and dogs have never been *simpatico*."

I looked over at Lockwood, who seemed to have simmered down some. "Sorry, Ross. The one we have is trouble enough."

"You guys are a lot of help." I risked another sip of coffee. "Thanks for the gedunk anyway, Cap." I saluted with my donut. I ate half and fed the rest to the dog. Queenan gave me an indignant look and grabbed another one.

We ate and drank in silence for a while until Queenan announced that it was time for them to go. He wiped sticky fingers on his pants leg, dropped his empty cup in the wastebasket, and they started out.

"Cap, hold up a minute."

Queenan stopped in the doorway. He looked at Lockwood, who nodded and continued toward the stairwell.

"I've been thinking about our talk at Hockman's," I said.

"Yeah? And?"

I listened for Lockwood to start down the stairs. "And I'm starting to get the idea that the Whitcanack twins didn't just pick my name from the Yellow Pages."

He pulled his hat brim down a little, dusted a few donut crumbs off his coat front, did everything but look at me. "I don't know what the hell you're talking about, Ross. But then I seldom do."

"Right. So what do you expect me to do from here?"

"Hey, far be it from me to tell you how you should run your game. But I guess if I were in your shoes, I'd just keep pulling at the threads."

"Even if it all came unraveled?"

He shrugged and looked at me. "What can a guy do?" He winked and sauntered away.

Chapter Eleven

After the cops left, I fooled around the office for a little bit longer, then I locked up, and the dog and I drove home. I thought about giving Mikey a call, but if he'd had anything to report, he would have let me know. I fed the dog his evening meal, and after a shower and a change of clothes, I was feeling refreshed and ready to forget about the case, the daily grind, and life in general for a while.

The sun was going down, and it promised to be one of those rare, cool summer evenings with a nice, easy breeze, so I put the dog and his water dish out back. He made a sulky face at me when he figured out I was leaving him there.

"It's just for a couple hours, pal," I said, giving his ears a quick massage. "Be a sport, and maybe I'll bring you back a hamburger." He wasn't appeased. He made a disapproving noise as I closed and locked the door, and he watched through the glass with big mopey eyes as I went through the house and out the front.

I drove over to the Buscadero. It really wasn't my kind of place, but Dusty and Pooter were still getting established, and I thought they'd be glad for the support. Anyway, since Dusty had dropped everything to lend me a hand earlier, I felt like I owed him the favor.

Almost right away, I regretted it. I'd gone there in the mood to have a quiet drink or two, but I'd forgotten how rambunctious cowboys could be even when they weren't primed with whiskey and tequila. This time the house was filled with them. They'd just finished a shoot at Republic and were all eager to turn a few days' pay into a night of rowdy fun. The music box was going full blast, but I could barely make it out above the racket of joshing, laughing, hooting and hollering cowboys.

As busy as it was, I didn't get to talk much to Dusty. Most of my time there, I spent sitting with Joe Lopez, another of the movie buckaroos and their resident expert on horse training. He was a nice fellow, and at first I was grateful he didn't try to talk horses with me, since I had no knowledge or interest in them. But he insisted instead on reminiscing about a case he'd helped me out on a year or so earlier. It had involved a pretty cowgirl singer, and it hadn't exactly ended well for me or for her, so I'd been doing my best to forget it.

Joe, on the other hand, seemed to remember it as quite an adventure and went on about it at such length that after my second drink, I made my excuses and left the place. I headed home in a pretty sullen mood. If the dog wasn't exactly the ideal drinking companion, he at least could be counted on to keep his memories to himself.

The first clue that things weren't right hit me—literally—when I opened the door. I was nearly knocked off my feet by a very large and excited dog. I knew I'd locked him in the backyard before I left. Yet here he was in the house, and I saw right off that his muzzle was sticky and wet with what looked like blood.

I took out my .380 as I surveyed the living room. It looked like the aftermath of an L.A. quake, with Jack the Ripper at its epicenter. Tables and lamps were overturned, pictures had been knocked from the walls, a chromium bar caddy had been dumped over and glasses and bourbon decanter—thankfully with its stopper still in place—upset. There were random splatters of blood on the furniture, the wood floor, the throw rugs, one wall. I quickly checked the dog over, not easy since he was still dancing around me in an agitated state. He had no injuries that I could see. Wherever the blood came from, it wasn't his.

Leading with the pistol, I followed a trail of blood drops into the kitchen. The lower half of the French door leading to the backyard had been smashed in. Broken glass and splintered chunks of wooden window frame littered the floor. It was clear enough how the dog had gotten in. The door was standing open, and the blood trail went through it, so whoever had run afoul of the beast had gone out that way.

I found a bedroom window open, and the screen cut, apparently where my uninvited guest had entered. The bedroom had been tossed, and there were signs they'd begun searching the living room before the dog decided to put the quietus on that. Nothing else appeared to be out of order.

I took a flash and checked the small back yard. I lost the blood trail about ten feet out, but the manzanita hedge along the back fence had a large gap in it as though someone had bulled through. The beam of the flash picked out something lighter in among the branches in the gap. I pulled it out. It was a tweed cap, a dingy tan herringbone pattern, missing its button on top. It was a man's size, and inked in crude letters on the cracked and stained leather sweatband was a name: E. L. Ballin.

I went back inside and cleaned the dog up with a wet cloth. He wasn't enthused about it, but while I worked at it, I ruffled his cheeks and told him over and over again what a good boy he was. That bought a little more cooperation. Afterward, I cooked him a little flank steak I'd been saving. I told myself he'd more than earned it.

It took me well over an hour to clean up all the mess and patch the broken door with cardboard. While I worked, I thought. Home burglaries in Los Angeles were not a rarity, and my neighborhood was no exception. But having just had somebody give my office the same treatment, I didn't think this was the everyday prowl job. Nothing was missing. Somebody wanted something I had. Or something they thought I had. I could see only two possibilities: the evidence in Whitcanack's death, or the blackmail book he may or may not have kept. Whatever it was, I was plenty steamed. Breaking into a guy's office was one thing, but his home was something else. And if they'd hurt the dog... As far as I was concerned, no matter what damage the big mutt did, E. L. Ballin had gotten off lucky.

Chapter Twelve

The dog had balked at being left behind at home, and after the excitement the night before, I couldn't blame him. He'd taken up his post in his corner of the office and was already napping, though it wasn't nine o'clock yet when Mikey came in carrying his satchel. I'd just sat down and was writing some notes.

"Morning, Nate," he said in a cheery voice. "Morning, dog." He squatted to rub the big mutt's noggin and looked up at me. "When are you going to give this guy a name, anyway?"

"He's not my dog to name." I sounded sharper than I meant to. I was getting tired of answering that question. Mikey ignored me. He went to his card table and started unpacking a few things from his satchel, whistling as he did.

"What's with you?" I asked after several minutes of the canary act. "You pick a winner at five-to-one, or what?"

He looked up with a proud grin. "I was gonna tell you when you were in a better mood, but since you asked...I got those prints developed from the hymn book. They came out nice and readable."

"Okay, that's good. And so...?"

He grabbed up some of the stuff he'd been unloading and carried it over. "They match prints I found on the whiskey bottle," he said. "They also match a couple of the lifts I took at the apartment. But here's the cherry: they *all* match the ones on Allen Whitcanack's fingerprint card."

I could tell Mikey was waiting for an 'atta-boy,' but even though it didn't surprise me, I wasn't so sure this was good news. What he was telling me was that my client's brother—also technically my client—had most likely murdered their father.

"That's good work, Mikey—uh, Mike," I managed to say. I guess it was enough for him—he started shoving print card after print card under my nose, insisting on showing me all the various points of comparison he'd found, and nattering on about accidentals and tented arches, whatever the hell those were.

I barely heard him through the racket in my brain. I was trying to compose inside my head exactly how I was going to pass this news on to Alanna and wondering if she'd even believe me when I did.

I was saved by the bell, in more ways than one, when the telephone rang.

"Ross, Bill Lockwood here." His tone was crisp and businesslike as always, but I didn't detect any edge to it. Maybe he'd gotten over wanting to wring my neck the day before.

"Say, Mac," he went on. "Before I get to why I called, a little bird just whispered in my ear that you had some excitement at Casa de Ross last night. They get anything?"

"Thanks to my—the dog, maybe tetanus and twenty or so stitches."

I couldn't figure how he knew. I hadn't bothered calling the cops. I *had* phoned Dusty and told him, though. I supposed he'd probably told a bar full of half-soused cowboys, and who knew who they told? For a big city, it never failed to amaze me how fast news got around.

"Glad to hear it," Lockwood said. "Maybe that dog's a keeper after all. But that's not why I'm calling. Got a couple of news items on this end."

"Okay, shoot."

"The lab report came back on the gun from yesterday. It did the dirty deed all right. Positive match for the slugs in Hockman."

"And?"

The pause was so long I thought the line had gone dead. "I probably shouldn't give you this part, at least not until we've made the pinch."

"On who?" My grip tightened on the receiver.

He blew out a breath. "Your anonymous client—one of them anyway. Alan Whitcanack."

100

"Shit." I hoped I sounded more surprised than I felt. "There's no question?"

"None. The prints on the rod couldn't be clearer and we have the Whitcanack kid's fresh from a drunk arrest a couple months back."

"What made you think to look at *his* prints?"

"Well, with the Whitcanack/Hockman connection…. Plus, the bluesuits turned up a neighbor who saw someone leaving Hockman's about a quarter to nine yesterday. A quote 'shrimpy, tow-headed, pansy-looking kid.' According to the wit, the guy drove off in a blue convertible with a gray rag roof. That all sound familiar?"

I swore under my breath. "Yeah, that's him."

"Listen, I can count on you, right?" he said. "Keep it under the hat, no little tip-offs?"

"Don't worry about me, Bill," I said. "I agreed to look into his old man's death, period. I didn't hire on to be junior's keeper." I looked at the print cards Mikey had laid on my desk. There was no point in staying cagey anymore. "In fact, you may as well know that it's looking like he's good for his old man's murder, too."

After another long pause, he said, "Okay, we can talk details on that later. I'll get word to you when we pick him up, but I can't guarantee if or when you'll be able to talk to him.

"I understand. I appreciate the call. And hey…"

"Yeah, what?"

"I know I was out of line yesterday. I should have—"

"Old news, pal. Old news."

"Thanks. Anything I can do on my end in the meantime?"

"You could talk to the sister, I guess. Without putting her wise, of course. We'll check the usual places, but if we come up snake-eyes, she might know where he'd be."

"She did tell me he likes to take drives up the coast."

"Anywhere in particular?"

"Not that she mentioned."

"Okay, that's worth knowing. I'll get word to the Highway Patrol and wire every police department between here and Monterey. Meanwhile, if she has heard from him, she's probably more likely to talk to you."

I wasn't crazy about putting one over on a client, but when she'd hired me, I'd made it clear that I'd follow the trail wherever it went. Her brother had committed a murder, and more likely two. My professional ethics could stand the stretch.

"Sure," I told him. "I'll brace her and let you know."

I left the dog with Mikey and drove over to the Hall of Records. I wasn't sure how to approach Alanna about Alan's whereabouts, but I thought I'd better do it in person rather than by phone. She might be less inclined to lie to me face-to-face, or at least if she did, I'd know it. It turned out to be a moot point. After being handed off like a football from one bored county drone to another, I finally spoke with some sort of quasi-supervisor—pasty-faced, doughy, and balding, with all the charm of ten-day-old bananas. He informed me in a phlegmy voice that Alanna had been out ill since the day before.

With her brother on the loose, that concerned me. If Alan knew he was a hot number—and he must have, since he'd already been lying low—it was possible he'd show up at Alanna's apartment. Not likely, maybe, but possible. With him running around and on the gun, I needed to get over there, but I thought it would be wise to take Dusty along.

I used the pay phone in the Hall of Records lobby and tried four times to call the Buscadero. I got a busy signal each time, so I gave up and called the office. Mikey picked up before the first ring died out.

"Listen, kid, Alanna's not here, so I'm going to her place to see if she's all right. Call the Buscadero and tell Dusty I'm on my way over. Keep trying him until you get through.

"Will do, Nate," Mikey said.

I was in the car and ready to head to Alanna's place when I realized I'd left my .380 in my desk drawer. I'd have to swing in and pick it up on the way to get Dusty.

The office was empty when I walked in. Both Mikey and the dog were gone. On my desk, I found a note in Mikey's neat handwriting. It said he had to leave and that the dog was downstairs at the diner with Benjy. The note didn't say if he'd reached Dusty. That would have annoyed me if I hadn't had more urgent matters on my mind.

I dialed the phone number for the Buscadero and strapped on my holster while the phone rang. To my relief, Dusty answered, so I wasn't slowed down by any of Pooter's pleasantries. Mikey had gotten through, and Dusty was waiting. I told him what was happening and that I'd had to make a stop but was on the way to pick him up. He told me not to bother—he'd borrow Pooter's car. I gave him the address and told him I'd meet him there.

When I approached Alanna's building, I could see that Dusty was already parked out front. Pooter's deluxe yellow Chrysler convertible was unmistakable—as large as a parade float and almost as ornate. I could see its polished chrome winking at me in the sun when I was still a block away.

I was sure that if Alanna did know where Alan was, she'd lie and deny if she already knew the cops were after him. In case she didn't know it, I wasn't about to tell her, but I needed a line she'd buy. I was puzzling over what it should be as I parked and met up with Dusty, and we headed up the walkway. I didn't see any blue Chevys on the street—I took that as a good sign.

I hadn't called ahead this time, so as we made our way up the little cobbled path, I glanced up toward Alanna's window, wondering if we'd even find her at home. The lights were on, and I caught a blur of movement crossing behind the curtains, so it looked like we were in luck. I didn't know why, but a moment later, something made me pause and take a second look. The curtains parted, and a figure appeared— not Alanna but her brother.

I signaled to Dusty, and we moved off the path and into the shadow of the jacarandas bordering it. I only hoped Alan hadn't seen us. I told Dusty to cut around and go through the courtyard so he could take the back entrance up, then I hurried inside. I hit the button to start the elevator down and made for the stairs, gun in hand.

I had no real reason to think Alan might harm his sister, but if he was in a blackout state, there was no guessing what he might do. Even in his right mind, he surely knew he was in a fix, which made him even more likely to get panicky and do something stupid.

The stairwell was one of those cramped jobs with a small landing where the stairs switched back on themselves halfway up. I double-timed it up them doing my best to make as little noise as possible. Just as I made the turn at the landing, I heard a gunshot and a thud from the floor above.

I took the second flight of stairs two by two and slammed through the door into a little vestibule. I peeked around the corner and down the hall. Halfway down, I could see the door to Alanna's apartment standing wide open with light spilling out into the softly lit hallway. I hugged the wall and cat-footed it in that direction listening for any noises from inside the apartment. Nothing.

I reached her door and was about to buttonhook in when something farther down the hall caught my eye. Near the end, where a right-angle turn led down another hallway, was a little sitting alcove on the left, which I knew from my first visit had a small sofa under a window. Two legs poked out into the corridor. A man's legs, motionless, in brown trousers and dark oxfords.

A tweed-covered arm and part of a white-blond head suddenly appeared above the legs. At the end of the arm was a gun. I ducked through Alanna's doorway as a shot rocked the narrow hallway. A bullet threw splinters from the door frame at about shoulder height. I stuck my .380 around and, with one eye, watched for the head to reappear. Instead, I heard the window slide up and the clang of hard shoes on a fire escape landing.

I swiveled my head around to scan the apartment, only long enough to note an empty room with nothing that looked wrong in any way. Then I hustled down to the alcove and the downed figure. Just as I reached it, Dusty came stampeding down the adjoining hallway in his chunky cowboy boots, his big Colt at the ready. I pointed toward the window and the fading clatter of steps on the fire escape.

I stowed my pistol and rolled the prone figure over as gently as I could, and my blood froze. Mikey Galvin. A second shock jolted me as Dusty's horse pistol boomed.

"Shit, missed him!" We heard an engine revving and tires squealing from the back street. A blue Chevy convertible, I was willing to bet.

I told Dusty to forget about it and to go check Alanna's and call for an ambulance. Mikey was bleeding from a hole high up in his chest on the right side, a couple of inches below the collarbone. From the blood flow, the bullet hadn't hit an artery, but that didn't make his wound any less deadly. I felt around behind his shoulder, and my hand came away clean, so the slug hadn't gone through.

"Jesus, Mikey," I said, more to myself than to him. "What the hell are you doing here?" I took out a handkerchief, balled it up, and pressed it against the wound as tightly as I could. It seemed to rouse him; his eyelids fluttered, and the green eyes darted around in confusion before settling on me and focusing.

"Sorry, Nate. I..." His voice was thin and sounded like it came from far away.

"No talking, kid. You just relax—help's on the way."

He gave a small nod and clamped a hand on my arm. "Alan," he wheezed out. "It was—" He grimaced and let go of my arm.

"I know, pal. Save it." I looked up as Dusty came back.

"Apartment's clear," he said. "No sign of the girl. I'm going downstairs to wait for the ambulance." He started away and then turned back. "I called the police. Told 'em she's missing and to tell Queenan their boy's armed and runnin' and in a shootin' mood."

I nodded, and he trotted down the hall. Mikey seemed to have passed out, but the bleeding was slower. I kept the pressure on and waited until Dusty came back down the hallway, followed by the ambulance crew and two bluesuits. It seemed like forever since he'd called them. At times like that, it always does.

Chapter Thirteen

I sat on a hard wooden bench in the waiting room, waiting. And waiting. I went into my pocket for a cigarette until I noticed I already had one burning, half-smoked, in my other hand. I stared at the motionless wall clock until I finally decided it must be broken, but when I looked at it again, forty minutes had passed. I'd tried calling Mikey's old man when we first arrived. He hadn't picked up, and I had no idea where, or even if, he was working.

I dropped another nickel in the pay phone in the corner and called Gus's diner. Benjy had had the dog for probably far longer than he bargained for, and I'd made arrangements with Dusty for him to take over. He was going to camp at my office in case Queenan or Lockwood called with any new information. I didn't exactly have hotel accommodations there, but Dusty was an old cowpoke and used to roughing it. The guy could sleep anywhere.

Gus himself answered the phone, and before I could even ask for his nephew, he was giving me hell in his gruff, Greek-accented way.

"Listen, Nate. What the hell you think, you bring this damn dog in my restaurant? You crazy in your head? This is not dog pound, this is fine eating place!"

That was a laugh. L.A. had more than its share of ptomaine palaces, and Gus's was well above their standards, but The Brown Derby it was not. I didn't have any inclination to argue the point or to listen to Gus going on at this rate, or at this volume, so I countered with some noise of my own.

"Gus. Gus Gus Gus Gus Gus." After the tenth or eleventh "Gus," the ranting paused.

"What?" he barked in my ear.

"I need to talk to Benjy." The angry voice went instantly conversational. "Sure. Why the hell you don't say so?"

Benjy came on the line in seconds and assured me that the dog had been no bother and he'd be happy to keep him anytime. He sounded a little blue when I told him Dusty was coming to take over.

After I hung up, I tried Floyd Galvin again. Still no answer, so I went back to my vigil on the bench.

Half an hour later, I was pacing the hall, still waiting for any update on Mikey, when I looked up and was surprised to see Alanna Whitcanack coming in through the outer doors. She looked around for a second and, when she spotted me, hurried over my way.

"Nate, I am so sorry," she said in a breathless rush. "I stopped by your office and your associate—Dusty, is it?—was there. He told me a boy who works for you had been shot, but not much else. Her agitation was clear. I wondered if it was because she suspected her brother was involved.

"Is the poor boy badly hurt?"

"Bad enough, I guess. The doctors haven't said much more yet. Where have you been? We've been trying to find you for a few hours."

"I had a doctor's appointment. I haven't felt well in a couple of days."

"Anything serious?"

Her face reddened. "Ladies' complaints," she said in a whisper. She put a hand on my chest. "But I don't understand how this happened. Why was the boy at my building? Was he delivering a message from you?" Before I could answer, she rushed on. "Do you have any idea who did this?"

I took a deep breath, took her by the hands, and led her to the bench I'd been warming earlier. She was watching me with frightened and confused eyes as we sat. Her normal self-assurance seemed to have taken it on the run, and I was even more convinced that she suspected the truth. But suspecting it and hearing it are two very different animals.

I wasn't sure how to begin or where to begin. Normally I'd have just delivered the blow straight out. But as protective as she was about her brother, I didn't know how it would go over. I didn't want her to throw a wingding, but I supposed that if she was so inclined, a hospital would be the place to do it. I decided there was nothing else for it but to just spit it out and come what may.

"Alanna, I'm sorry to tell you this, but it was Alan who shot the boy."

She stared for a good five seconds before she flashed a brittle smile that never quite reached her eyes. "But that's absurd. No. You can't possibly think that Alan would—"

"I don't think it. I saw him, Alanna. He shot at me, too."

She passed a skeptical eye over me as if the absence of bullet holes proved me a liar. "No, that's not possible. There must be.... You must be—"

"He was in your apartment, Alanna. I don't know if he intended to hurt you, or was looking for help, or—"

"Help? Help with what? Is Alan all right?"

"I can't say. He ran, and we don't know where he is. The police are out there now trying to find him."

"Police?" She held a white-knuckled fist to her mouth. "Why?"

"I told you, he shot Mike—the boy." I rubbed her wrists and tried to keep my voice as calm and soothing as I could, though there was nothing soothing in the words I had to say. "He, uh, shot someone else yesterday."

She was just staring at me by then, her eyes wide and mouth half open. I wasn't even sure she had heard me. "The milkman," I went on. "The man who found your father."

"Is he..." she almost whispered. "Is he...?"

"He's dead."

Her eyes rolled upward and closed tight as she threw her head back and leaned away from me. I held onto her wrists—I thought she was about to keel over in a faint. But her head came back level, and when her eyes opened again, her face held an expression of eerie calm.

"Tell me the truth, Nate," she said in a flat, lifeless voice. "Did Alan kill our father?"

As much as I wanted to, I couldn't dodge it. "I'm afraid it looks like he did," I said.

Her calm expression stayed fixed for only a second or two. Then her eyes pinched shut, and her mouth opened wide, and from deep inside her came an ungodly, unearthly howl. The few other people nearby moved away, and a couple of others coming down the long hallway did a quick about-face.

I held Alanna until the gale-force yowling changed to a thin coyote wail. As it died away, she started breathing in and out through her nose, puffing like a locomotive, while her shoulders jerked with violent, silent sobs.

After five minutes—or hours—had gone by, she ran out of gas at last and pulled away from me. She pawed her tears away with both hands and spoke in a weak, tired voice. "You have to promise me you won't let them hurt him. It's not Alan, you see. It's not his fault. He doesn't even realize…." She took a tight grip on my arm just as she had that first day in my office.

"Promise me," she said again.

"I'll do what I can. But a lot depends on Alan. Meanwhile, you can't stay at your place."

She scoffed. "But I'm not in any danger."

"We can't know that. You said yourself, Alan may not know what he's doing."

She seemed to yield to the logic in that. "All right. If it will ease your mind, I'll take a hotel room." She wiped her eyes and face with a handkerchief and took out a little pocket mirror. Studying her face in it, she half laughed, half sobbed. "Good Lord, what a mess!"

People were starting to move down the hallway once more, relieved the storm had passed. "I suppose I'd better go see about that room," Alanna said when she'd touched up her makeup and put her stuff away again. "I'll call and let you know where." She stood up, adjusted her attire a little. "I do hope your employee will be all right." She gave me a half-wave and made her way to the doors.

Sometime later, I'd burned one cigar down to my knuckles and was thinking of lighting another when Queenan walked in and strolled my way, leaving his own trail of cigar smoke.

"How's the kid doing?" he asked.

I shrugged. "So far, so good," I said. "Surgery went fine, and they've got him in a recovery room."

"Those youngsters bounce back. He'll be okay, you watch. And then he's gonna get plenty mileage out of this."

"How's that?"

"He'll have one hell of a story, and a beauty of a scar to show off. The girls won't be able to keep their hands off. And you know guys his age—all they think about is how to get their beans snapped."

"I don't think he'll be up to getting his bean snapped for a while."

He waved his cigar. "Blah. When I wasn't much older, I took a bullet in the spring and was back on the job by summer."

"Where'd you get hit?"

He gave me a look. "I just told you, in the spring."

I wasn't feeling much like joking. "Did you come by just to crack wise and tell war stories, Cap?"

"Nah, I called your office, and Hoot Gibson told me you were still here. I figured you'd want to know that the junior Whitcanack's still in the wind. Lockwood's out on the prowl as we speak. And no sign of the sister, either. She ain't come home."

"She was just here an hour or so ago."

"Yeah? So, safe and sound, I take it?" I nodded. "Where the hell's she been hidin' out?"

"Doctor." I laid a hand over my lower belly.

He flashed me his palm like a copper stopping traffic. "Enough said. I still got a detail watching her place."

"She won't be back tonight, anyway. I told her she should go to a hotel. She just paged me here—she'll be at the Belmont over on Hill Street."

"All right. Well, I guess I'll keep the boys on her crib anyway, in case her idiot brother comes sniffin' back around." He looked at his watch. "I better get back out there myself and give Lockwood a hand. Stay in touch, Ross."

"Will do."

Shortly after Queenan left, a doctor came out and told me that surgery had gone without a hitch. He said the slug they'd pulled out was a soft-nosed .38 and that the kid was lucky; it had gone through his chest muscle and flattened against the scapula without hitting any arteries or doing any major damage. I felt a little better about things after hearing all that, but still wasn't going to be at ease until Alan Whitcanack was either locked up or dead.

I hung around a while longer, hoping maybe I'd be able to see the kid, even if he was still doped up. I must have dozed off on the bench—I woke up to a nurse shaking me awake to say that they were moving Mikey out of recovery. She gave me his room number and said that visiting hours started at eight if I wanted to check in on him in the morning.

Before leaving the hospital, I tried calling Floyd Galvin one last time but still couldn't reach him. I felt guilty about it—he deserved to know—but I was also relieved. He was bound to blow his stack when he found out and would most likely want to go to town on me. I couldn't blame him for that, but it had been a long day and I wasn't feeling much like tangling with angry parents.

With nothing else I could do there, I headed for my car. I knew Dusty was an early to bed, early to rise type of guy, so I didn't go by the office on my way home. I was confident he and the dog were both in good company.

I had a tough time getting to sleep. After the day it had been, I should have been plenty tired. Too much on my mind, maybe. Plus, although it had only been a couple of nights, the house was weirdly quiet without the sound of the snoring dog.

Chapter Fourteen

I hit the hospital at eight sharp, but the nurse on duty told me Mikey was still sleeping. Not unusual, she said, in a case like his. She suggested I try again around noon. "Everyone's awake for lunch," she said brightly.

I drove from there to the office to see how Dusty and the dog had gotten on. Fairly well, from the look of it. Dusty was leaning back in my chair with his feet on the desk and was poring through my copy of Judge Fricke's *Criminal Investigation*. His cowboy bedroll was neatly rolled up and tied and standing on end in the corner.

The dog greeted me at the door with bright eyes and a big smile, his tail flapping like a metronome. By the way his fur was matted down on one side, I could tell he'd just been sleeping. Dusty, of course, was wide awake and cheerful, two early morning traits foreign to my nature.

He was sipping a cup of coffee from Gus's and pointed a boot toward another cup on the corner of the desk. "Have you some coffee, Nate. Oughta still be hot."

I tossed my hat on the desk and sat in one of the guest chairs. I tried the coffee. Not as lava-hot as the stuff at Gus's usually was. I was thankful for that.

"So, how did you two jaybirds get along last night?"

"Aw, he's a good old hound," Dusty said. "We did fine. Except for just one thing."

"What's that?" I was hoping it was nothing too serious. I had a busy day ahead and was planning to try and wangle a bit more dog-sitting.

Dusty laid the book aside and lowered his feet to the floor. "That dadgum

112

kid in the diner downstairs. Benny."

"*Benjy*. What about him? Benjy's a good egg."

"Oh, he's a nice young fella, all right. But you know what he was feedin' this dog when I went in there to pick him up? Salami."

I didn't know a lot about dogs, but I was pretty sure salami wasn't toxic to their breed. "Yeah, so?"

Dusty screwed up his face until his big handlebar mustache nearly brushed his eyebrows. "You put half a pound of salami through a canine digestive tract, you know what it comes out the other end smelling like?"

I was getting the idea, but he'd never forgive me if I didn't ask. "What?"

"Salami!" He slapped a palm on the desk, and the dog hurried to his side, wondering what new game was afoot. Dusty took off his big hat, which never came off indoors except in the presence of ladies, and fanned the air with it. "Lord have mercy. You ain't got enough windows in this place to chase *that* stink out. I burned up every match I had and a whole box of 'em I found in your desk." He grinned and ruffled the dog's fur. "Tried to choke ol' Uncle Dusty to death, didn't you, you ornery booger?"

I tried not to laugh. I thought I'd detected a faint aroma in the air when I came in, but I hadn't mentioned it. I had my doubts how much of it was really the dog's doing.

Before I could think of a snappy retort to Dusty's complaint, he went serious on me. "How's our boy?"

"Okay, I guess. Still sleeping it off when I got there. I'll check on him again later."

"He'll be just fine," Dusty said. "He's young and full of piss and vinegar, and he's gonna come out of it with a dandy story to tell."

"Jeez, you sound just like Queenan. But I hope you're both right. Listen, I hate to ask, but—"

"Say no more. I figured you'd need me to watch this big fella a little while longer. Already squared the morning with Pooter."

"Thanks."

"Only thing is, he's got to head out to the Iverson Ranch on a picture this afternoon. So I can only be here until two o'clock. I could watch him longer, but it'll be at the bar."

"No, two's fine. I just need to take care of some business I didn't have time to get to yesterday."

"Sure you won't need a hand?"

"I don't think so. I just need to go talk to Charlie Dubek. I've got a sneaking suspicion he can tell me who broke in here and tried to feed himself to the dog at my place the other day."

"Well, I'll be here if you need me. I always can leave the pup with Benny again, so long as he promises no more salami."

I saw Dubek's big, black Cadillac in the lot alongside his building, so the boss was definitely in today. I'd intended to go straight to him but decided he'd maybe be more likely to level if I had something more in my corner first. I parked and walked back through the lot to where a big, open, roll-up door led into the main print shop.

The sound inside the cavernous shop was deafening, and the smells of grease, ink, and warm paper were thick in the air. I had to give Dubek his due—the size of the operation was impressive. Rows and rows of presses clattered away, some automated and some operated by an army of ink and sweat-stained pressmen while printer's devils ferried huge cans of ink back and forth. Other workers, many who looked like high school kids, were busy hand-setting type from large, flat wooden boxes with myriad compartments. Three huge linotype machines chugged out lead slugs with entire lines of type, many of them more than a foot long.

As I made my way through the maze of machinery, I got quite a few curious looks, but none of the workers stopped what they were doing to ask my business. I'd made nearly an entire circuit of the shop when I spotted a familiar face. He was leaning over a table near one of the doors that led into the office, giving two young printers an earful about a job that was apparently not done to his satisfaction. He waved a sheaf of printed sheets at them and stabbed a greasy finger at it here and there while he ranted.

He was Eddie, the chimp-faced redhead I'd seen in Dubek's office. He was nearly the only one in the entire shop whose head was bare. The others wore cloth caps of one style or another, almost to a man. His left hand, which clutched the botched printing, was wrapped in gauze bandaging, wound nearly to his elbow.

He didn't see me approaching. When I was near enough to be heard over the din of the place, I pulled the rolled-up tweed cap from my inside pocket and called out, "Eddie Ballin!"

He turned with an irritated glance to see who'd had the nerve to interrupt his tirade. I waved the cap at him. "You dropped your lid, pal." I could see he was a slow thinker, but when he caught on, his eyes shot wide, and he obeyed the natural instinct of his kind. He ran. He was fast for a little fireplug of a guy—he managed to make it through the roll-up door and halfway across the parking lot before I tackled him.

"Get off of me, you lousy bastard!" he said in a muffled voice. I had him pinned down with my knee in his back, and his good arm torqued up behind him, his face half planted in the gravel. After questioning my parentage, he went on at some length about my perceived personal habits and preferences, hygiene, and relationship with various breeds of farm animals.

I paid his colorful insults no mind. They told me what I already suspected. Although he tried to put up a front as a hard boy, Eddie Ballin was not. A true tough guy wouldn't feel the need to resort to schoolyard slanders. A true tough guy wouldn't have run.

"Well, Eddie," I said as he grunted and strained in his panicked struggle. "I'm glad to see your mouth's in full working order. Because we've got a lot to talk about."

"Like what?" He tried to look at me but couldn't twist his head around far enough. "I don't even know you, mister."

"Is that right? So do you always start haulin' ass when total strangers call your name?"

About then, I heard voices in the distance behind me and looked back to see two or three of the printers standing outside the open door and craning their necks our way. One of them was one of the kids Eddie had been reading the riot act. They all laughed, elbowed each other, and went back inside to their work. Eddie didn't seem to be a favorite.

"Look," he said. "I don't know what...I don't know...can you get off me, please? This gravel's hot."

"You bet, pal. The minute you lay off the bullshit and tell me what I want to know."

"You ain't told me what you want to know!" He was almost wailing in his protest.

"You know what? You're right. I'm sorry. I got so distracted with hearing your take on my family history, I guess I forgot."

"I didn't mean nothin'."

"I'm sure. We'll skip that for now. What I want to know's pretty simple, and I'll use nice, short words. Why did you break into my office and my house? What were you after?"

"You're nuts," he said. "You got the wrong bird here. I ain't no burglar, I'm just a foreman in a print shop. Why the hell would I—" He stopped talking when the cap landed on the ground inches from his nose.

"Are you telling me I've got the wrong E. L. Ballin? Boy, that sure would be embarrassing. But if I do, gee, I'll be happy to apologize and go on my way. Say the word."

"I don't know nothin' about no break-ins."

"Yeah? What happened to your arm?"

"Pinched it. Caught my sleeve in the gears of one of the platen presses."

"Well, that's a nifty story, Eddie. Of course, it's bullshit, but I'll give you credit for trying. Here's the thing, though." I shifted my weight and twisted the bandaged arm behind him. He cried out in pain. "I don't have time or patience to play this game with you. So you give me some answers, or I'm going to finish what my dog started, maybe tear this arm right off."

"But I told you, I ain't never—"

I gave the arm a twist, and he yowled like a catfight. "All right, all right! Let up, willya?"

"It's up to you, pal. You going to answer me or not?"

"Yeah, yeah. Just get off me first."

I backed off him and stood up. He rolled over and sat up, clutching his wounded arm to his chest. He started to stand.

"You're fine where you are, Eddie."

"Aw, have a heart. I told you, this gravel burns."

"Then snap it up. Tell me your story, and you can get back to bullying teenagers around."

He looked up at me, and his shoulders slumped in defeat. "It was the boss."

"The boss. Dubek?"

He nodded, then looked up again with alarm in his eyes. "He ain't gonna know I told you this?"

"You give me the straight dope, I can keep it between us pals."

He looked unsure but went ahead. "He said you had somethin' belonged to him, and he wanted it back."

"Somethin'? You can do better than that, Eddie." I reached for the arm, and he flinched.

"A book—he said you had a book."

"What kind of book?"

"A little red book. Kind of an address book. I dunno."

'What else did he tell you?"

"That was it, I swear. I was just supposed to go in, find the book, and bring it to him. That's all I know."

"What did he do when you didn't find it?"

"He was hot. I mean *hot*. But what could I do about it?" He held up his bandaged arm. "Hell, I tried, didn't I?"

I asked him a few more questions, but he didn't seem to know anything else of value. I believed him—he was a beaten man.

"Okay, Eddie," I said at last. I held out a hand and helped him to his feet. "Dust yourself off and go back to work. Just one more thing. I find out you lied to me, or I get any kickback because of our little talk, and I'll come back and visit you again. And next time, I'll bring my dog along, maybe let him work on that other arm. You take care now."

He didn't say anything. He just nodded once, then turned and ambled back toward the print shop.

The secretary looked up from her typewriter as I walked in. She gave me the stock greeter's smile.

"Mr. Van Overschelde, good morning." She may have had all the personality of a damp dish rag, but I had to give her credit for being a pro. Even I had forgotten that moniker by now. She looked at an open book on her desk and frowned. "I don't seem to have you on the calendar," she said. "Would you like to schedule an appointment?"

"No time for that now. I've got urgent business with Mr. Dubek."

"Well, I'm sorry, but his calendar is completely full this week."

"That's okay. I won't be long."

I moved around her desk, and her fingers clawed at the air like she was going to try and grab hold of me. I started legging it double-time down the long, stifling hallway, and I heard her heels thump-thump-thumping on the carpet behind me as she tried to keep up.

"Mr. Van Overschelde, really...you can't just...Mr. Dubek is not.... He's in a meeting with his attorney."

By the time I'd reached the padded door, she was fairly gasping for air. I shouldered the big door open, and the secretary crowded by me, eager to get in the first word.

"I'm sorry, Mr. Dubek, he just pushed his way past me," she said.

Dubek looked up from his desk, annoyed at the intrusion. Across from him, with his back to me, sat a little silver-haired guy with narrow shoulders. When Dubek saw it was me, there was a flicker in his eyes, then he smiled with amusement.

"It's okay, Gladys. Mr. Van Whatshisname and me are old pals. You can leave the door open—Mr. Coombs was just leaving."

Gladys beat a grateful retreat, and J. Martin Coombs turned to give me a curious, owl-eyed look through his pince-nez. He stood as I came fully into the room, courteous to a fault.

Dubek turned to him. "Marty, I guess we're all done for now. Looks like my next appointment's a little early."

Coombs's poise faltered just a fraction. He stood stock-still for a beat, then turned his head and murmured to Dubek, plenty loud enough for me to hear, "Frankly, Charles, I would deem it best that I remain to allay any—"

"Nah, nonsense," Dubek said in a jovial way. "I'm sure you got things to do." He came around the desk, laid a big mitt on the shyster's shoulder, and all but propelled him to the exit. "But thanks for comin' in, Marty." The last I saw of Coombs as the huge door closed behind him was a nervous flash of that tiger shark smile.

Dubek slapped the back of Coombs's chair as he moved to sit behind his desk again. "Rest the dogs, Ross, and tell me what's got you in such a rush today."

I pointed a thumb over my shoulder. "You sure you don't want your mouthpiece to sit in?"

"That weasel? He don't need to know all my secrets. He'd sell 'em tomorrow to the highest bidder. And I'm guessin' you're here to talk secrets. They're a gumshoe's stock and trade, right?"

"I'm here to talk about burglary. My office, my home."

"Sorry to hear that. I didn't read nothin' in the papers about it."

I tossed Eddie's cap on this desk. "Maybe you can read that instead." He flipped it over and read the sweatband. "Looks like your foreman's been doing some moonlighting," I said.

"Then maybe you oughta be havin' your talk with him."

"I thought I should go to his boss first."

A slow smile crawled across his face. "Don't bullshit me, Ross. You think you can pull a Red Grange on my own lot, and I ain't gonna hear about it?"

"Red Grange was a halfback. I don't know how much tackling he did."

He blew out breath in an I-don't-care sound. "So Eddie's little hobbies involve me how?"

"How about *you* don't bullshit *me*. Math wasn't my best subject in school, but I can add two and two."

"Meaning?"

"Meaning I have a talk with you that steers to the topic of Cecil Whitcanack's blackmail book. You tell me there's no such animal, that it's just a—what did you call it? A *fever dream*. Then presto, somebody puts the prowl on me, twice. Not just somebody, but the guy you pay to push kids around in your shop. I'm not a big believer in coincidence, are you?"

119

He didn't make any reply. He just sat and studied me through half-lowered eyelids.

"Now, Eddie's not much," I went on, "as crashers go, but he did a pretty thorough job. Or he did until my dog mistook his arm for a hambone. But both times, he left without getting what he came for. And that's not because he's an imbecile. I mean, don't get me wrong—he *is* an imbecile. But the reason he didn't find it is that I don't have it. I've never had it. And I'm not looking for it. So now that you know that, maybe you and your trained monkey can stay out of my hair."

He continued to stare at me for a long time. I could see he was weighing a decision.

"Tell you what, Ross," he said. "Let's say for laughs that I have a clue what the hell you're talking about. If Whit had something like that book, I would have done my damnedest to talk him out of usin' it. A thing like that— like I told you before, a guy would be playin' with fire." Without asking, he poured two tumblers of Scotch and slid one across to me.

"And if I thought he'd left somethin' like that behind when he kicked off," he went on, "you can bet I'd try to find it. But not to use it for myself. To burn the damn thing. Because sooner or later, a hot potato like that would be sure to get somebody killed."

He took a long taste of his Scotch. "Now I've played straight with you, Ross, so I'm gonna believe you're doin' the same. So if you're tellin' me, one right guy to another, that you never had such a book, I'll take you at your word. And I'll even whisper a little sermon in Eddie's ear. Trust me, you won't have no more trouble outta him."

"Fair enough." I'd said what I came to say, and it seemed like he'd gotten the message. I was anxious to get to the hospital and try again to see Mikey. I started to get up, but Dubek held up a protesting hand.

"You ain't gonna drink your Scotch?" He stabbed a thick finger at my glass. "Buddy, that's twelve-year-old single malt, eight bucks a fifth. I don't pour this stuff for every mug that comes through the door."

Five minutes wouldn't matter. I sat back and picked up my glass. I saluted him with it and took a healthy dose. I'd forgotten how good it was.

"So tell me," he said as he refilled his own glass and took a swig. "How's things goin' with your case on Whit? Suicide, or did somebody chill him?"

I took another gulp of the Scotch and felt it warm me all the way down to my wingtips. "Come on, Charlie," I said with a grin. "You expect me to buy that the next police commissioner of our little hamlet doesn't have plenty of ears downtown already?"

He made a comical face and shrugged. "So the kid's really good for it, huh?"

I nodded and finished my drink. "Looks like it." I put my hat on and stood to go. "Thanks for the Scotch."

"You like it? I'll send you a bottle."

I touched my hat. Just for fun, I asked, "I don't suppose *you* know where Alan's hiding out?"

He lifted his glass, rotated it in front of his face, and watched the light play through the amber liquor. "No, I don't, but I'll tell you, Ross, and this ain't no lie. If I did know, I wouldn't tell you. Not 'til after I paid the little pantywaist a visit myself. And then I'd do my first official act to trim the police budget—I'd save the coppers the price of a bullet. Like I told you last time, Whit was a friend."

Chapter Fifteen

With the long night and the early morning, I hadn't eaten anything since the day before. Having only black coffee and Scotch in my stomach didn't make me feel any too hot. I decided to give Mikey a little extra rest and go to the office first, to relieve Dusty early and to treat him to lunch at Gus's.

Dusty and the dog were both eating cheeseburgers when I walked in. The dog's was sans bread and accoutrements and Dusty's was piled so thick with lettuce, tomatoes, pickles, and onions I couldn't make out the meat.

"That Benny don't know much about dogs," Dusty said, with his mouth muffled by a fist-sized bulge in his cheek. "But danged if he can't cook a burger!"

"I'm happy to see you two enjoying yourselves." The dog had wolfed his patty down almost whole and, seeming to have only then noticed that I'd come back, trotted over for a petting. "Any word from Queenan or Lockwood?"

Dusty shook his head. He finished chewing and swallowed the mass with some effort. "*Nada.* And we been here the whole time —the boy brought the food up."

"Well, I was planning to treat you to lunch, but since *Benjy* beat me to it, I guess I'll eat alone." I slapped the dog's rump. "You mind watching him and minding the phone while I grab lunch?"

He pulled out his old pocket watch and squinted at it. "Nope. I said I could look after him until two, so take your time. You look like you could use it. Before you head down—how'd things go with Dubek?"

"I don't think we have to worry about any more sneak thieves."

Gus's was empty of customers except for its two perpetual patrons, two old geezers who occupied the far corner booth. They were as much fixtures in the diner as the red leatherette stools, the glassed-in pie case, and the cash register. I'd never come to Gus's, night or day, that I didn't find them installed in that same booth and talking nothing but horse racing. At the moment, they were engaged in a heated debate about the various tracks up and down the coast, from Tanforan to Tijuana.

The only other occupant was Benjy, who was sitting on a stool behind the register, reading the *Times*.He was a thin, medium-sized, handsome kid, twenty-five or so. He had dark hair and ink-black eyes, and a longish nose with a distinct bend in it. I didn't know whether he'd broken it or it had just grown that way— I'd never asked. Although I'd known Benjy for the five years I'd rented the office over the diner, and I considered him a pal, I didn't know much about him. He was Gus's nephew, I knew that much. I knew he was in college, although his course of study was kind of vague, and he'd been pursuing it for longer than I'd known him. And I knew he liked talking local politics. But that was about it.

I took a booth and told Benjy to fix me up with a meatloaf sandwich and a tall glass of milk. He looked suspicious as he set the milk down. I didn't usually drink the stuff, but I thought it would do my stomach good. I smiled to myself, thinking about how strange it was that Benjy knew my habits while try as I might, I couldn't even recall his last name. I wasn't sure whether that said more about him or me.

"Gus around?" I asked when he brought my food.

"Nah, he went home to fight with my Aunt Sophia."

"Fight about what?"

"Who knows?" At least I'd be spared any more harangues about the dog, on this visit anyway.

"You think you could watch the dog again for a couple of hours? Dusty has to leave soon, and I'm going over to the hospital."

"Sure, boss, glad to. I doubt Uncle Gus'll be back today" He set the plate down. "How's Mikey doin'?"

"Not bad, considering, I guess. I haven't been able to see him yet."

I promised Benjy I'd say hello for him, and he left me to my meal. While I ate, I thought about Alanna Whitcanack. With Alan on the hook for their old man's murder, that pretty much wrapped up the job she'd hired me for. But with Alan out there doing a crouch, I was still concerned for her. After the hospital, I'd go over to the hotel and make sure she was okay. Then if I hadn't heard anything in the meantime, I'd pay Queenan and Lockwood a visit to see if they'd had any luck finding their man. I wasn't ready to ring the bell on the Whitcanack case until Alan had been tapped out of the fight, one way or the other.

Mikey had weathered the night okay, and the doctors said he was going to be just fine. It would take him some work, and maybe another surgery, and his right wing wouldn't be a whole lot of use for a while, but they said that in a couple or three months, he should be as good as new.

I'm not sure what I expected to find when I walked into his room, but other than the bandages and sling and the fact that someone appeared to have combed his hair with an egg beater, he looked about as pink and perky as any other day.

He had some magazine or other open on the tray in front of him and was so engrossed in whatever he was reading he didn't look up when I came into the room. He probably thought I was just another staff person bringing one more pill or shot his way.

"Hey there, Hopalong Cassidy."

He looked up at my voice, and a huge grin split his face. It faded just as quickly. He dropped his chin to his chest and looked at me with sheepish eyes. "I guess you're mad at me, huh?"

I pulled a chair up beside the bed and sat. "Well, I'll admit," I said, "I'm half tempted to drag you out of that bed and whomp your skinny ass, but considering where we are, I think you've already been punished enough for your sins. Still, I've gotta ask. Just what the hell were you thinking?"

He looked down and picked at a loose thread on his blanket. "I don't know. I thought it might take you a while to get to Dusty. I was just going to watch her place until you guys got there." He proceeded to lay out the whole story, as much as he could remember:

He'd ridden the streetcar to the stop near Alanna's and taken up a position at the nearest corner. It allowed him to watch the front entrance to her building. After ten minutes of seeing nothing, he got bored and moved inside to have a look. A typical rookie's blunder, I thought, but I didn't say so.

He found the little reading nook on her floor and thought it would be an ideal vantage point to watch her door from. No sooner had he settled on the sofa than he heard a noise from back down the hall and saw Alan Whitcanack coming from the stairway. Alan walked straight to Alanna's door and opened it with a key. After he went in Mikey wasn't sure what he should do. He didn't know whether Alanna was home. He tried listening for any telltale sounds but was too far from the apartment.

He finally decided to creep down the hall and listen at the door.But the moment he moved out of the alcove, the apartment door opened and Alan stepped back out. Their eyes locked, and Mikey said he figured he must have had a look of recognition on his face because Alan started toward him, reaching into his coat pocket as he came. Mikey's recollections became a little fuzzy at that point. He vaguely remembered being on his back and Alan standing over him with a gun in his fist. Alan pointed the gun at Mikey's head, he said, but then turned and fired a shot down the hallway. After that Mikey recalled me talking to him as he lay there. His next memory was of waking up in the hospital with a bad taste in his mouth and the sickly-sweet odor of ether in his nostrils.

When he'd finished, Mikey looked at me and shrugged. "I guess I just wanted to show you that I was good for something other than boring stuff like prints and photos."

"You showed me, all right. And damn near got yourself killed for it."

"Sorry."

"And so you know, those boring prints of yours are what put the finger on Cecil Whitcanack's killer. So maybe, for now, you ought to stick to what you're best at. Trust me, buddy, I know that doesn't mean it's all you're good for."

I felt bad. I'd come to see how the kid was doing, maybe cheer him up, and

I'd ended up lecturing him instead. To change the subject, I pointed at the tray. "What are you reading?"

"Medical journal. One of the docs loaned it to me. It's got an article by a Swiss doctor who's doing research on people born without fingerprints. Says he thinks maybe it's congenital."

"Jeez, when did you start using ten-dollar words?"

"It just means—"

"I know what 'congenital' means, wise ass."

"Well, anyway, it's pretty interesting stuff."

"I don't know. I think I'll continue to take my crooks *with* fingerprints, thanks anyway. So, how long are they keeping you?"

"A few more days, I guess."

"How'd your old man take the news?"

He grinned. "He had murder on his mind to start with. I won't tell you what all he called you. But I finally got it through his head that it was all my fault and that you didn't even know. He's still plenty mad, but now it's at me." He rolled his eyes. "What else is new?"

"So at least now I don't have to sit with my back against the wall. Think he'll get over it?"

"Oh, yeah, he'll forget it in a week. Anyway, I've only got to put up with him until September."

"You're still going off to Berkeley?"

"It's the best criminal science school in the country. And the doctor says I should be okay to travel by then if I go easy." He laughed. "It's not like I was gonna go out for the football team anyhow."

We sat and made meaningless chit-chat for a while. He started to look tired, so I told him I needed to get going.

As I was walking out, he said, "Hey, Nate?" and I stopped. "At least now I've got a nickname. 'Bulletproof Mike.'"

"I don't know, kid," I said with a stifled laugh. I pointed at his sling. "I think there's some pretty convincing evidence to the contrary."

I started out again and once more heard, "Nate?" I stopped and turned again. "Are you gonna keep the dog?"

"Yes, *Michael,* I'm keeping the dog. Get some rest."

I parked on my same bench in the hospital corridor for a minute to collect my thoughts. Since I still hadn't heard anything since last night, I didn't know whether Queenan and Lockwood had run Alan Whitcanack to ground yet. I hoped they had. I was debating whether I should look them up to see where things stood or drive over and check on Alanna first when I became aware of someone standing over me. I got to my feet, expecting it was another one of Mikey's doctors with a progress report.

It wasn't a doctor. It was a balding, bespectacled guy in a rumpled seersucker suit. If I hadn't been expecting somebody else, I'd have known him right off, although we hadn't crossed paths in several years.

"Nate Ross," he said, "Boy, last time I saw you, you were still in county greens."

"Hello, Ray." I shook the hand he offered. "What brings you around?"

Ray Pinker ran the crime lab for L.A.P.D., and there wasn't a sharper bird in his profession. The city boys, homicide dicks in particular, couldn't have closed a fraction of their cases without the work that Ray did behind the scenes with his test tubes and microscopes and cameras and the way he had of dazzling judges and juries with the mind pictures he painted of the scenes he worked. He had a way of making them feel like they were seeing the crimes for themselves.

"I heard Mike Galvin caught a bullet," he said, "so I thought I'd come and see how he was faring."

"You know Mikey...uh, Mike?"

"Yeah, he's a student in a couple of classes I teach." He smiled. "Lately, he's more like my shadow. Never seen a guy so keen to learn. Hell, I think he spends more time in my lab than most of the boys who work for me. He's always dropping by with a batch of questions or to talk about something he's read. Fingerprints, ballistics, fiber analysis, poisons...he soaks it all up like a sponge." He laughed. "I tell you, give that kid five years, and I'm going to be afraid for my job."

I'd known Mikey was an eager beaver about all this lab stuff, but I never

127

had him pegged as a star pupil. I wasn't about to ask Ray, but I was betting he was "the guy" who'd furnished Mikey with Alan Whitcanack's fingerprint card.

"He'd mentioned he was working for you," Ray said, "but I figured he was just...." He checked himself, maybe worried about sounding too accusing. It wouldn't have mattered; I was kicking my own ass plenty already.

"Yeah, he wasn't supposed to be shadowing anybody," I said. "He does tamer stuff for me—document research, fingerprint work, photo developing, and so on. But he's a hard kid to keep a bridle on."

Ray laughed. "I'll bet he is. So, how is he doing?"

"Good as can be expected," I said. "The docs fixed all the damage, but he's got a long road before he's close to a hundred percent again. You know how gunshots are."

"Yeah." He nodded and looked thoughtful, maybe a little worried, behind the specs. He waved a hand toward the bench. "Say, you got a minute?"

"Sure." I'd always gotten along with Ray and was glad to see he didn't seem to share the general low opinion of me that most of the coppers he worked with held. Although we'd fallen out of touch, in no time we were shooting the lemon like old pals. I caught him up on what I'd been doing since leaving the sheriffs, and he asked a few questions about a couple of the cases before he got around to what he wanted to talk about.

"The rumor downtown," he said, "is that you're taking a second look at the Whitcanack suicide." I nodded, and he went on. "Between you, me, and the fence post, none of my guys ever got close enough to that one to say if it *was* a suicide."

"So I heard."

"We got the word from on high that Whitcanack was a done deal, and our talents weren't needed. I had to go to the coroner's and see for myself, though, when I heard the guy had no fingerprints. I'd read about cases like that but never thought I'd see one, let alone two."

"Yeah, that's pretty strange—wait. What do you mean *two*?"

"Yeah, Pasadena coppers went out on a dead body call the other day," he said. "Another Colorado Street bridge jumper, I guess. Anyway, I haven't

128

had a look yet, but I hear through the grapevine this guy had no prints either. What are the odds? It could only happen in L.A., right?"

After another minute or two of small talk, Ray said so long and headed down the hall to see Mikey. And I headed out to follow a hunch.

Chapter Sixteen

It was late in the day, and I was happy to see that Doc Reese didn't keep banker's hours. He looked up from a microscope when I came through the door. "Ah, there's the boy! No need to tell me why you're here."

"Come again?"

"You've heard about our recent John Doe." He gave me a wink and a knowing grin. "I knew you'd come around. I can always spot a fellow connoisseur of synchronicity."

"Synchronicity?"

"It means—"

First Mikey, now Doc. If people kept explaining words to me I might get a complex. "I know what it means," I said. "It's just...never mind. Can I get a look at this one?"

He noticed my empty hands and gave me a disappointed look.

"Kind of in a rush," I said. "I didn't have time to stop. I'll owe you a box, okay? It's important, Doc."

"All right. Nobody's identified him yet, so he's not going anywhere."

I followed him into the huge walk-in refrigerator where Doc's patients resided before and after their turns on the cutting table. He pulled out one of the long, narrow drawers and drew back the white sheet.

The body on the steel tray was clearly male, but its outward appearance didn't give much else away. The extremities were more or less intact, although one arm was shattered and the shoulder far out of joint. The trunk was flattened and split and shapeless, with splintered rib ends poking through in places. The head was caved in on one side, and only a few broken teeth near the center of the pulpy mass in front showed that there had once been a face there. The wisps of hair that clung to the crushed skull were darkened with all the stuff that had once been inside it, but a few random strands appeared to be whitish blond.

"Jumper?" I asked when Doc had covered the grisly mess and slid the drawer back in place.

"You'd think it, wouldn't you?"

"What do you mean?"

"Well, they did pick this one up down in the arroyo, under the Colorado Bridge. And he *did* clearly take the plunge. But that's not what killed him."

"No?"

"No. To put it in plain English, somebody pounded the bejesus out of his face and head and dropped his body over the side. I guess they thought a hundred-and-fifty-foot drop would disguise the damage they'd done, and we'd write it off as just another suicide."

"Jesus. I guess it's no wonder nobody's i.d.'d him."

"Maybe. But we haven't even had any inquiries. Nobody looking for someone missing who fits the description. Now that's curious, don't you think?"

I did think. "Who found him?" I asked.

"A couple out walking their dogs came upon him late Tuesday morning. I put time of death between ten p.m. and midnight Monday."

"And this guy has no fingerprints?"

Doc shook his head. "Just like the other one. Whitcanack. This fellow's haven't been removed, either. They were simply never there."

I thought about synchronicity and what Queenan had said about coincidence. And he was right. This could hardly be coincidence. I thought about those strands of light hair.

"How old was he, Doc?"

"No more than twenty-five, if that."

"You happen to have his clothes handy?"

"I do." He went to a ceiling-high rack of shelves on the wall. They were filled with heavy cardboard cartons, each with a numbered paper tag attached.

131

He selected one, brought it over, and set it on one of the steel tables. "All he came in with was the clothes on his back," he said. "No jewelry, nothing in his pockets, no identifying labels in the clothes."

He lifted the lid. The clothing was folded as neatly as its condition would allow. A once-white shirt, a tie, a gray flannel suit that looked neither expensive nor cheap. No hat—not surprising. The coat had a sleeve torn loose, and it and the shirt, in particular, were matted and crusted with gore.

When I lifted the suit and trousers out, I suddenly knew how a yegg feels when he hears all the safe's tumblers click into place and the door swings open. In the bottom of the bin, underneath all the gruesome mess, was a pair of shiny black Congress gaiters.

"I gotta go, Doc," I said. "But I'll pay you another visit soon to bring you those cigars. And when I do, I'm pretty sure I'll be able to tell you who your John Doe is."

I needed to go back to the Whitcanack house, but first stopped by the diner to relieve Benjy of his canine charge. He'd spent a lot of time looking after the dog, and I didn't want Gus to give the poor guy an even bigger dose of guff over it than he'd already given me.

The diner was empty of people again except for Benjy and the two old track punters. They were quiet this time, both their noses buried in racing forms. Benjy, meanwhile, was sitting on a stool at the far end of the counter, apparently teaching my furry roommate to shake hands. The kid looked up and grinned as I walked over.

"He's a smart pup, this guy." He held out an upturned palm to the dog. "Show him, boy. Shake! "The dog plopped his hairy paw into Benjy's hand, and they both turned and beamed at me. "See that? I only been working with him for half an hour.' He tousled the dog's ears. "What a good boy!"

"Yeah, that's gonna come in handy," I said. I looked back toward the kitchen. "Your uncle ever come back?"

"No, he lost the fight with Aunt Sophia, so he's home cutting the grass and fixing their broken fence.

Good news for both Benjy and me, if not for Gus. "Well, I'll take the dog off your hands now. Just got one more stop to make before I call it a night."

Benjy looked disappointed. "Okay, well, anytime you want me to watch him...."

"I appreciate it, and thanks a lot for today." I took out my wallet and slipped out a ten spot.

Benjy frowned at the bill and me in turn. "You can just put that right back in your pocket. What's a pal for?"

"Okay, you're the boss." I put both the sawbuck and the wallet away. "Thanks, kid." To the dog, "Come on, mister."

When we were halfway out the door, Benjy called out, "Hey, I keep forgettin' to ask."

I stopped. "Yeah?"

"What's his name, anyway?"

"See you around, Benjy."

We went upstairs so I could collect a couple of things I was going to need. The dog curled up on his blanket, and by the time I was ready to leave, his lips were fluttering with heavy snores. He looked so peaceful I didn't like to disturb him. It was safe enough to leave him—he'd already proved he could be trusted not to ransack the place. Let him sleep. I could pick him up on the way home.

It started raining on my way out toward Highland Park. It was one of those Southern California summer rains that come with no warning from a clear blue sky, with big, warm drops plunking down a foot apart, the smaller ones in between evaporating before they had a chance to hit the ground. It went on for fifteen minutes, then stopped as suddenly as it had started. It left the air smelling fresh but feeling like the inside of a Turkish bath.

The key for Whitcanack's house was still under the back mat. The house looked no different than it had the last time I'd been here. It didn't look as if Dubek had made another run at it. He'd probably thought it was a waste of time since he'd been convinced that I had Whitcanack's book. Maybe after our talk earlier, he'd give it another go.

The mood I was in, I couldn't have cared less whether Whitcanack was hiding crooks out from the law, or blackmailing them, both of the above, or none of the above. I didn't give a damn where his little book of secrets was, or if it even existed, or whether it was nothing but a fairy tale.

All I cared about at that moment was that a kid who worked for me—a good, decent kid—had been shot. Although it looked like he would survive it, nobody could say yet what it would mean for his future. And I now had a pretty good idea who had done it. And they needed to pay.

I found it hanging right where I'd seen it when I'd been here before. It was on the wall above the mantel that held, among its other family treasures, the mortal remains of Althea Whitcanack. The frame was plain. Grainy, reddish wood—mahogany, maybe—about ten inches high and a foot and a half wide. Behind its glass insert was a cream-colored plaque made of plaster of Paris. A line of gilt paint divided it down the center from top to bottom, and each side held, in a smaller gilt metal frame, the photograph of a smiling, tow-headed child. Their names were painted underneath. Alan was on the left, and Alanna on the right. At age four or five they had looked, if possible, even more alike. The matching outfits added to the similarity—he wore a vest and shorts, and she wore a flouncy dress of identical plaid. But it wasn't really the photos that interested me. Next to each one, pressed into the plaster, were the tots' handprints.

The plaque was hung high up on the wall, so I had to pull an ottoman over and stand on it to take it down. I took the plaque into the kitchen, where the large windows on adjoining walls allowed the remaining daylight to spill in. I bent the nails on the back of the frame that kept the plaque in place and carefully lifted it out. I laid it on the table, then opened up Mikey's print kit satchel, which he'd helpfully left in my office when he got the wild hair up his ass that had sent him on his little scouting trip to Alanna's.

I had to give the kid credit—Mikey was nothing if not organized. Along with all his powders, brushes, and other fingerprint paraphernalia —neatly stored in their own compartments—in an inside pocket the satchel held his notebook and a folder containing the various print cards he'd collected while helping me out on Whitcanack. Each card was carefully labeled with dates, times, where it was obtained, and the name—if known—of whose print was on it. As fascinated as I was with these examples of the kid's skill and professionalism, that wasn't the stuff I was looking for just then. I found what I wanted in a big, white envelope inside the notebook: the L.A.P.D. fingerprint card he'd gotten from his "secret" source.

I laid the print card out next to the plaque and took out Mikey's jeweler's loupe. I'd rather have used the big magnifying glass I kept in my top desk drawer, but I'd have felt pretty silly driving across town with that in my pocket. A private eye packing a magnifying glass—such a pulp magazine cliché.

I'd have been much better off if I could have brought Mikey or Ray Pinker along, but without those options handy, I set to work as best I could. I was far from an expert at this stuff, but I'd been around it enough to get the basic idea. I figured Nate Ross could follow spirals and squiggles as well as the next guy. I went to work comparing the prints on the card to the ones on the plaque. It was a little tricky since those were quite a bit smaller. But I squinted through the loupe until my eyeballs felt like they were both in the same socket, and my neck and shoulders were cramping. After over half an hour of checking and double-checking, I was convinced my hunch was right. While Alanna's tiny fingerprints had all the normal ridges with their various loops and whorls, Alan's were featureless blanks, just as Doc Reese had described his father's. The inked prints on the print card from Alan Whitcanack's arrest didn't belong to him. They belonged to his sister.

I knew my amateur league analysis would never hold up in any court, but I had a strong suspicion things were never going to come to that. I replaced all Mikey's stuff in his satchel, then put the plaque back in the frame and bent the nails back in place.

Out of respect for the late Whitcanacks, the Mrs. if not the Mr., I carried the keepsake back into the living room to return it to its spot on the wall. Climbing onto the ottoman again, I looped the wire back over the nail in the wall. It wasn't hanging quite level, and when I stretched a little to set it right, the ottoman wobbled underneath me, and we both took a tumble. Trying to catch myself as I fell, I caught a sleeve button on the rim of the brass urn.

It toppled off the mantel and hit the floor with a crash. The lid from the thing cartwheeled across the room and ended up under the armchair where I'd seen Dubek ruminating. The urn did a couple of barrel rolls in the other direction, spilling poor Mrs. Whitcanack, or what was left of her, out across the polished wood floor.

"Well, shit." I picked myself up, dusted a little Althea off my pant leg, and was about to go looking for a whisk broom when something in the overturned urn caught my eye. A squarish shape, half-buried in the remaining ash and chunks of I didn't like to think what else.

I dug the thing out and saw that it was a book. Pocket-sized, bound in red cloth. Before I'd even opened it, I knew what I was looking at. I laughed out loud, though there was no one there to hear me.

"Cecil, you sneaky son of a bitch."

I tried calling Queenan from Whitcanack's house, but the telephone service had already been cut off. I guess the utility companies read the obituaries just like everyone else. I'd decided it could wait until I was back at the office.

I heard the dog whining and pawing at the door when he heard me coming down the hall. I wondered if he needed a nature break, even though I'd given him one not ten minutes before I left him. When I unlocked the door and went in, I understood his agitation right away. Someone had been at my door, and they'd slipped a plain white envelope through the gap underneath. Inside it was a folded piece of thick stationery paper. I unfolded it and read the message written on it in a hand that was surprisingly steady. It said,

> *Nate,*
> *Come to the Colorado Street bridge and bring the book. Come alone.*
> *If you don't, the next time you see me, I'll be on a slab.*
> *Lila*

Chapter Seventeen

The familiar blue Chevy was parked near the middle of the bridge in the gap between two of the sets of twin electroliers. Its gray top was still wet from the brief rain and almost glowed in their reflected light. I parked well back from it between another set of lights. I cranked the window halfway down so the dog would have air, and I told him to stay.

I moved down the sidewalk toward the convertible, and when I got closer, I could see the outlines of two figures in the back seat. When I was twenty feet away, the door opened, and Alanna Whitcanack stepped out. The Harlow wig was missing, and she wore a stylish felt hat over, from what I could see of it, was short, mannishly cut, white-blond hair. She was holding a stubby black revolver pointed at the other person in the car. When I drew a little nearer, I could see it was Lila Porter.

"That's close enough for the moment, Nate," Alanna said. "Take out your gun—don't tell me you don't have one. Take it out slowly, otherwise...." She cocked her head toward Lila.

I held my hands away from my body. I slowly reached back and, with thumb and two fingers, lifted my .380 out by the butt end. I'd have given everything to have someone, anyone, drive by at that moment, but the light traffic I'd been grateful for on the drive over had stopped working for me.

"All right," she said, "come slowly this way and hand it to me." I took a step, and she repeated, "Slowly." She pushed her gun a little more in Lila's direction.

When I was close enough, Alanna snatched the .380 from me, flicked her eyes over it, and then shoved it into a pocket in her skirt. Up close, I could see that Lila's hands and feet were tied with scarves.

She looked out at me with a tear-streaked face. "I'm so sorry, Nate. She made me write it. She—"

"You shut up," Alanna barked. Then to me, "Is the boy dead?" She asked it as though she were asking me for the time.

I answered her through clenched teeth. "No."

"I'm *so* glad. He's the only real innocent in any of this."

"But you shot him anyway."

She ignored me and motioned with the gun. "Get in."

"What's the game here, Alanna?" I was pretty sure of the answer, but I thought Lila and I both had better odds if I could keep Alanna talking out here.

She smirked. "The game's over now, I fear. I knew it when I saw those police buzzing around my apartment building like gnats. I'm tired of it all. I'm tired of trying to guess what they know, what you know. I'm tired of your continual digging, digging." She took a deep breath and blew it out. "I'm tired of keeping secrets…so many secrets. But since I don't know how much the police have or what you've told them, you and I need to talk." I opened my mouth, but she shook her head. "In the car. Front seat."

She shifted her aim to me and backed into the car next to Lila. I got in the front seat as she pushed her gun's muzzle against Lila's ribs.

"Close the door," she said.

"It's pretty hot in here."

"Roll down the window, then."

I did as she insisted and turned in the seat to face the two women. Lila's face was pale, but she looked at me with steady eyes.

"All right," I said. "Hail, hail, the gang's all here. What is it you want to talk about?"

"Lots." She smiled a disquieting smile. "But first, I want you to give me the book."

"Book. You mean the hymnal? It's at my office. We found Alan's prints—well, yours—in it. But you knew that already, didn't you?"

"Don't try and be cute, Nate. I mean my father's book. I'm sure you've found it. You can hand it to me now, or I can take it off your body after I shoot you both." She twisted the muzzle in Lila's ribs for emphasis.

"Fine, you win. It's in the glove box of my car."

She took a quick look back. "All right, then, it's safe enough for now. We'll get to it in a bit."

"So it was all about that little red book? Your father, your brother, everything?"

"My father deserved what he got. He betrayed me after all I'd done to help him along in his little enterprise."

"With the birth records, right? Working at the Hall of Records, it was a cinch for you to pull birth records to furnish his clients with new identities."

She threw her head back with pride. "You're only half right. The records for people still living were useless. I'd start with death records. Of people—ideally infants—born near the same year as the client."

"Why infants?"

"Because they had no other public record. Only birth and death. No school records, no licenses, no military service. And once I destroyed their death records—"

"Quite a nifty scheme."

"Yes, and without me…." She was getting flushed with agitation. She paused a moment to calm herself. "I was essential to it, but my father and Charlie Dubek still claimed the lion's share. They treated me like an employee, not a partner. When I learned my father was making even larger sums by blackmailing our clients, I felt even more badly used. He assured me he was doing it 'for the family.' For our future. Mother had died by then, and he said all the money he was putting away would pass to Alan and me when he was gone. Then a couple of months back—" The rage rose in her again. She pressed her lips together and looked out the window. I tensed, waiting for a chance at her, but she seemed to sense it. She turned to me, bug-eyed and panting, and pressed the gun to Lila's temple.

"Sit back!" she shrieked. I sat back.

"What happened a couple of months ago, Alanna?" I asked as gently as I could.

She breathed in and out through clenched teeth like a sprinter. As her breathing slowed, she spoke in a forced, unnaturally ordinary tone. "We had a terrible fight. And he told me that…that he was cutting me out, that he was going to turn it all over to Alan."

"Why?" Her head tipped forward, and she looked at me under her eyebrows, eyes shifting back and forth and seeming not to focus.

"Why did you fight, Alanna?" I asked again.

Her voice was very small and childlike. "Because." I waited for more, but it didn't come.

"Because," Lila spoke up in a surprisingly calm voice, "he'd found out it was you. You locked Alan in that ice box years ago."

"I told you to shut up," Alanna said. Her face darkened, and the fury rose in her like steam in a boiler. "I told you to *shut up!*" She pushed the gun into Lila's forehead. "Say one more word, and I'll kill you, you bitch! I'll *kill* you!"

I opened the car door. It was all I could think of to distract her. It worked. The gun swung from Lila to cover me, and Alanna hissed, "Close that door and sit back."

I did, and she stared at me with hard, hot, crazy eyes, crazier for the sudden smile that split her face. The gun swung back to Lila.

"It was a good plan, you know? The police never even knew I was a girl. I pretended to be drunker than I was, and I gave them Alan's name when they took me in and fingerprinted me. When they let me out in the morning, I laughed all the way home. Then it was just a matter of waiting. Waiting for the right time. I went to see my father. I told him I'd come to apologize, to make amends. He'd been brooding and drinking and wouldn't listen, but he was too drunk to send me away. I had Alan's gun and was going to shoot him with it then, but…." She stopped with a puzzled frown. She looked at me. "You said 'your father, your *brother*, everything.' How did you know that Alan's dead?"

"His shoes," I said. "And his fingerprints, or lack of them."

She snorted. "Just like our father. Freaks of nature, the two of them."

"John Doe 'suicide' from the canyon right under this bridge," I said. "What did you do, sap him out and do a tap-dance on his face before you fed him over the side?"

"More or less." She giggled. "I used a hammer. He'd been an albatross around my neck long enough. If everyone thought he killed our father and disappeared, I'd be in the clear and free at last. The mousy little bastard could finally repay me for all the years I spent looking after him."

"So why didn't you use his gun? On your father, I mean?"

"The old man was so drunk by then that he thought I was Mother, and it got me thinking. I suggested we go for a drive like we used to, and I helped him to the car. I fed him more whiskey until he passed out, and then I started the engine and left him." She looked at me and bobbed her head up and down. "It was better that way, you see? No telltale gunshot to bring the neighbors snooping. I left enough fingerprints that Alan would be blamed anyway. And even if they did rule it a suicide, at least then everyone would know my father had died a coward."

"Why the hymnal?"

Her smile was wicked. "That song was a favorite of my mother's. She'd play it over and over. It would have mortified her. It served her right for snitching on me. She wrote it all down in her diary, the stupid woman. Can you imagine? She kept my secret from Father all these years only to tell him after she was dead."

"Why Hockman?"

She shook her head. "Who?"

"The milkman."

"Oh, that. He came to the house that evening to collect his bill, and since Father could barely stand, I answered the door. He was very curt, this man, so I told him to come another time. I thought it was a good joke—Father would be dead then, and he'd never get his money. Served *him* right for being rude.

"You killed him because he was rude?"

"Of course not." She said it in an indignant huff. "But it was just my bad luck he was the one who found Father. First, he mucked up my plan by wiping away my fingerprints. Then he called me at work and said that if I didn't pay him, he'd tell the police that I'd been there that night." She giggled again. "So Alan's gun came in handy after all."

Her face looked dreamy for a moment, like she was enjoying happy memories, then it turned serious once more. "Now, if you're finished with all your silly questions, you can start answering mine. How much have you told the police? What do they know?"

"Does it really matter now?"

"I don't know," she said, stamping her foot like an impatient child. "How can I know until you share with me what they have?"

"Suppose I'm not in the sharing mood?"

She drew a circle in the air with the gun's barrel. "Then my father loses his wife, his life, and his fiancé." She looked at Lila and smiled. "Oops. *Ex*-fiancé."

I wasn't inclined to tell her what she wanted. It wouldn't do me or Lila any good—I was sure of that. But I figured she had the same plans for us either way, and the longer I could keep her talking about that, or anything, the better the odds I'd get a chance to trip her up.

"They don't know Alan's dead," I said. "And they don't know that Alan's fingerprints were really yours."

"How did you know that, by the way?"

"The plaque on your parents' wall. Six or sixty, your prints don't change."

She shook her head. "I suppose you think you're terribly clever."

"Not really. It's not so hard to outwit someone who's out of her wits."

"And yet here we are. I've won."

"Maybe so. We'll see."

She pointed the gun back at me and gestured toward the door with it. "Now, that's enough talk. Let's collect my book. Carefully."

I climbed out. She had me back away out of striking range while she got out. "Walk to your car," she said. "Very slowly. Reach in with one hand only. Get the book and bring it back, and no nonsense, or I *will* shoot her." She aimed the gun at Lila again.

I walked back down the sidewalk as she watched. I'd had the book in my inside pocket the entire time; I was only angling to get to the car. I opened the passenger door and made a show of keeping my right hand on top of the door frame. I leaned in as though reaching my other hand for the glove compartment and slid the book out of my coat pocket. I stood back up and showed Alanna both hands, the book in my left.

She motioned for me to come back, keeping the revolver trained on Lila. I started back, not bothering to close the car door. When I reached the Chevy again Alanna grabbed the book from my hand and told me to stand over against the bridge railing. With her gun to Lila's head and keeping me in sight, she untied the scarves around Lila's ankles and wrists and had her step out and stand on my right.

Alanna held the gun down low and trained on us as a couple of cars drove by. When they were out of sight, she frowned at the gray residue on the book and looked up at me. "Where was it?"

"With your mother's ashes."

"Of course." She laughed. "I suppose he assumed we'd find it when we added his."

"Or maybe never find it at all." She frowned again at the notion. "What's the plan now?" I asked.

"For you two?" She placed the book on the back seat and took my gun out of her pocket. She switched it with her own, which she laid down next to the book. "Murder/suicide, I think. You shot her and tossed her over, then followed her down. A Romeo and Juliet ending—the newspapers will love it. You're sure to make page one."

"Cute. But I meant about the book, now what?" I was hoping to get her talking again. If she was talking, she wasn't thinking. "Are you planning to pick up where your old man left off, bleeding more on-the-lam crooks dry?"

"Certainly not. What my father was doing was foolhardy, even though it was lucrative, very lucrative. Too dangerous. Charlie told him so. That's why I needed to find the book first—Charlie wanted to destroy it. But father hid away the money he'd already made with it." She reached back and picked the book up again. "He'd heard about the banks in Switzerland that allow secret accounts, total confidentiality." She shook the book at me with triumph. "He wrote the account numbers in here as well."

"Yeah, about that...."

"What?"

"If you're talking about that page in the back with all the numbers on it, it's gone."

For the first time that evening, her eyes looked clear and lucid. "Gone?"

"Yeah, it's gone. Before I came out here, I tore it out of the book."

An uncertain smile flickered across her face. "You're lying. You're just trying to buy time."

I shrugged. "One sure way to find out."

She glared for a second or two, then held the book up in the light spilling from the streetlights. Keeping the .380 on us, she shifted her eyes from the book to us and back as she turned pages with a thumb.

When she reached the spot near the back and found only a ragged edge where the page should have been, her jaw set, and her eyes glittered with malice. She dropped the book.

"Where is it?" she spat. I gave her a hearty smile in response. It infuriated her—pretty much what I'd had in mind. She advanced on me, eyes blazing. I sidestepped away from Lila, and Alanna moved with me, pointing my gun at the middle of my face.

"You tell me where it is, or I'll kill you this instant."

"You do that, and you'll never find it. You'll lose it all."

She shifted the gun to her left hand and aimed it at Lila. "Then I'll kill *her*."

I let the smile dissolve and glanced back over the bridge railing. "Lady, you shoot her, and you'll sure as hell have to kill me unless you can fly."

She stood glowering and gnashing her teeth and hissing like a cobra. When she opened her mouth to speak, there were little bubbles at the corner of her mouth. "I came to you for help," she said. "For *help*. And now it's all ruined. *You've* ruined it. All this is your fault. *Yours*, you son of a bitch!"

With the gun still trained on Lila, she raised her other fist in anger. She started pummeling me with it in the chest, the shoulders, the face. As she lashed out mindlessly, she wailed over and over, "Where is it? Where is it? Where is it?"

She was making such a racket she didn't hear the sound coming from the direction of my car. A faint, scratching, scuffling noise that grew louder and faster as it drew nearer. Too late, she saw a flash of movement to her right and turned her head. I took that opportunity to bat her left arm down, and my gun clattered to the concrete. Alanna's eyes shot wide in disbelief as eighty pounds of charging, snarling, furious red canine launched at her.

His teeth looked even more deadly in the artificial light. He slammed into her, bowling her over backward, and clamped an arm between his powerful jaws. She screamed and flailed as he wrung the arm back and forth, shredding cloth and flesh in his frenzy. Droplets of blood and saliva spattered the pavement around them like summer rain.

I scooped up the gun and waded into the fray. I grabbed the dog's collar. "It's okay, boy. It's okay. Let her go." He had a bad case of tunnel vision, and it took quite a lot of tugging and coaxing on my part to pull him off.

When I'd managed, Lila rushed over to Alanna and started using the scarves she'd been trussed with five minutes earlier to bandage the torn and bleeding mess the big dog had made of Alanna's arm. I guess I'll never understand women.

I collected Alanna's gun from the convertible and tried to put the dog back in my car, but he was having none of it. I walked him back over and settled for looping the handle end of his leash over one of the Chevy's window cranks. It wouldn't be nearly strong enough to hold the big bruiser, but with any luck at all, he didn't know that.

If I'd thought the mauling had taken the fight out of Alanna, I was wrong. While I was getting the dog situated, she suddenly shoved Lila back, scrambled to her feet, and made for the railing. Sometime back, in an effort to stop jumpers, the city had topped the bridge's concrete balustrades with wrought iron fencing five or six feet high. Before I could reach her, Alanna was scrambling up and over the vertical rails like a demon monkey.

She winced and cried out as her makeshift bandage snagged on one of the curved-in spear points at the top of the fence. The scarves tore loose and fluttered away down into the deep canyon. She slid down the other side and stood gripping the bars and peering between them at us like a jailbird. Blood coursed down her damaged arm and ran down the cold metal.

"Do you suppose it's true, Nate?" she called out. "What it says in my mother's old hymn? If the wheels of nature bring the night of death, do they

145

really also bring eternal day?" She smiled one last time. "You said it yourself. There's one sure way to find out."

She threw her head back, and with a wild, piercing laugh, she let go of the bars and vanished from view. Her laughter was still echoing off the canyon walls when she hit bottom.

Chapter Eighteen

"Don't know if Lockwood mentioned yet about Dubek," Queenan said. We were standing at the bridge railing, looking over the side at the crew working far down in the canyon. I didn't envy their job. Watching the volleys of flashbulbs popping among the oaks and sycamores down there was like seeing lightning through clouds.

"What about him?"

"You'll like this. Billy and me got the buzz while we were out beatin' the bushes for the Whitcanack kid. Our patrol boys in Highland Park caught a call earlier, hysterical woman screaming. Big ritzy house up on Mount Washington. Dubek's place. The woman's the housekeeper, babblin' out of her head so's they can't understand a thing she's sayin'. But she leads them into the library—"

He barked a short laugh. "Can you feature that? A mug like Charlie Dubek with a *library*." He leaned a shoulder on the railing and flicked cigar ash between the bars. "Anyway, there the big ape himself sits at his fancy desk, with a hole in the back of his head and what little brains he had spread out all over the blotter."

"Well, I'll be damned. There goes my bottle of Glenfiddich, I guess." I watched as the crime scene guys down below started packing away their gear, and the wagon started to drive away, taking whatever was left of Alanna Whitcanack to her appointment with Doc Reese. "I guess the mayor's gonna have to look around for a new commissioner."

Queenan took Alanna's short .38 out of his coat pocket. "And dollars to donuts I got the murder weapon right here." He sniffed at the revolver, put it back in his coat. "Jeez, Ross, you ever wound up a case where anybody in it was left breathin'?"

I looked over at Lila, sitting on the back seat of Lockwood's car, talking through the open door with him as he finished taking her statement. "I don't know, Cap. I'd say the right people stayed above the turf, and the right ones ended up under it." Then Alan Whitcanack crossed my mind, and I felt like a chump for saying that. So I added, "Well, mostly, anyway," It wasn't much, but it wasn't nothing.

"But as long as we're talking Dubek," I added, reaching into my own coat pocket, "Here's another piece of evidence to add to your collection." I handed him the small red book.

He looked confused for a second, then his eyes lit up. "You gotta be shittin' me." He started flipping through the book, his ugly smile growing broader with every page he turned. "Good God all Friday! The fugitive detail boys are gonna have more work than they can stand." He stopped when he noticed the torn-out page. "What gives here?"

I shrugged. "Search me."

He gave a shrug of his own and turned a few more pages. He let out a low whistle. "There's some big-time names in this baby. This is front page all the way, pal. For months."

"Who knows?" I said. "Maybe there'll be another promotion in it for you."

"Blah." He fanned the air with his cigar. "Captain's my last stop. I ain't so fond of kissin' municipal ass I wanna go no higher." He looked over to where Lockwood and Lila seemed to be wrapping it up, handed the book back. "Tell you what," he said. "You give that to Billy. He can bring it in. It was his case to start with, anyway."

I put the little book back in my pocket. As I did, I felt a nudge at my hand and looked down at the dog. He'd been sitting beside me, and he gazed up at me with his big wet eyes. In those eyes, I read total loyalty and trust. If I ever met a human who looked at me like that, I might have to rethink my attitude toward my species.

With the goofy grin back on his face and his tongue lolling out, he didn't look much like the demon beast he'd been no more than an hour earlier. I scratched between his ears, and he closed his eyes while the grin stretched even wider. One back paw thumped the concrete in time with my scratching.

"I'd say your partner there's the real hero of the day," Queenan said. "I guess now you're pretty happy you decided to play Nate Ross, Defender of Motherless Mutts. No doubt he's the brains of the outfit, too." He leaned over to give a pat. "Ain't that right, boy?" The dog jerked his head back and lifted a lip to show the big copper a fang or two. Queenan snatched his hand back and gave us both the evil eye. "You two are made for each other."

The ambulance boys had looked Lila over, but she'd insisted she was fine. Once Queenan and Lockwood gave us the go-ahead, I offered to drive her home.

The three of us piled into my Ford, the dog in the small back seat. He wasn't pleased with the arrangement, but he took it like a champ. Before we'd gone half a mile, he was stretched out to his full length, fast asleep.

Lila was silent for the first part of the ride. I didn't try to force any conversation—she'd had one hell of a night, and I was sure she needed some quiet time. But as we tooled down Figueroa with the soft summer night air blowing in through the wing window, she turned to me. "I'm sorry I lied to you."

"About what?"

"About Whit, and why he broke our engagement. I didn't really lie, per se, but I didn't tell you the whole truth. But, you see, it was Whit's secret, and I told myself it should stay hidden, that I owed him that much." She took out a handkerchief and touched the corners of her eyes with it. "Whatever bad things he was involved in—and please believe I didn't know about any of that—he'd always treated me well. But I know now that I was wrong not to tell you."

"You can tell me about it now, if you want."

She twisted the handkerchief between her hands. "Whit had found his wife's diary when he was sorting through her things, and he read what she'd written. About Alan's 'accident.' He was devastated. He'd never been very much of a father to Alan, you see, and now that he knew the truth, he didn't see how he could ever make that right. Plus, he didn't know what he was going to do about Alanna. But he told me he cared for me too much to ask me to be part of such a broken family."

She looked out the window for a long time before she spoke again. "Maybe... maybe if I had told you all this before...."

I wasn't sure what I could say to her. The only thing I could come up with was what Lockwood had said to me. "That's old news, kid. Old news."

She lived on a quiet little tree-lined street in Highland Park, not more than a mile or two from the Whitcanack place. I knew the neighborhood—I'd known a family who lived there when I was a kid. To try and distract her from any more dark thoughts, I started telling her about growing up in Glendale, our neighborhood, my school days. I stayed away from the topic of my own father, figuring that wouldn't do her any good.

She seemed easier by the time we reached her neighborhood. She even laughed when the dog let out a long, stuttering fart, and I cranked the window down so we'd survive it.

"What's his name, anyway?" she asked as she turned to look at the snoozing animal. "Your dog."

I was about to give her my standard answer when we made the last turn, and my headlights raked her street's sign. *Monte Vista.*

I had to smile. "Monte," I answered. "His name's Monte."

Chapter Nineteen

I saw Lila again a few days later. It wasn't anyplace nearly as swanky or intimate as the Biltmore. She'd come to the funeral for Alan Whitcanack. They held it at the Hollywood Cemetery, just across from where Alan had lived. Since the Whitcanack clan had gone into extinction, Cecil's boss, Herm Bausch, had ponied up for a burial with all the trimmings, and Lila came with him to pay her respects. She looked good, considering the ordeal she'd been through. She looked sad, but nobody looks jolly at a funeral. When they drove up, and she saw me standing over by my car to have a last smoke before the service, she walked my way.

"I didn't expect to see you here," she said with a melancholy smile.

"Herm Bausch called to tell me about it. I guess I figured it was the least I could do." I was about to confess the real reason I'd come was that I'd hoped I'd see her there, but I held back. It didn't really seem like the right time or place. "Do you know if...?" I hesitated. I wasn't sure she was the person I should ask. But she gave me a questioning look, so I marched on. "I was just wondering if they're burying his father alongside him."

The smile didn't dim. "No, Whit's being cremated tomorrow. Herm saw to that, too. There's no funeral, but afterward, I'll take his ashes to the house. He'll be back with Althea."

She teared up a little at the last. I was ashamed that my first thought was that I hoped I'd done an okay job cleaning up the mess I'd made in the house. To cover, I said, "The key's under the back mat." Then I immediately felt like a mug for saying it. She saved me by laying a hand on my arm.

"Would you mind if I sat with you?"

151

"No," I said, "I'd like that." People were filing into the little chapel by then, so she took my arm, and we followed.

It was a nice service, I suppose, as those things go. I've never been much for funerals. No matter who's being planted or what kind of life they lived, everybody pulls the long face. People stand up and say a lot of things about the deceased that anybody who knew them well enough to be there knows are half bullshit and only half the story. I always thought the Irish had the right idea for sendoffs: have a few drinks, tell some stories, sing a song or two, bust up the furniture, then move on.

Still, Alan's service was dignified, and they managed to keep the hoopte-doodle to a minimum. I'd only met the kid the one time and had heard him say no more than a fistful of words then, but I suspected that he'd have liked the finale. I wasn't clear on whether the bird in the suit officiating was a real clergyman or just one of those guys they throw in as part of the package deal, but he ended his eulogy with some familiar words.

Ye wheels of nature speed your course; ye mortal powers decay.

Fast as ye bring the night of death, ye bring eternal day.

The wheels of nature hadn't been all that kind to Alan Whitcanack. All anybody could hope for him was that he was in a sunnier place at last.

As we walked from the graveside, I offered to drive Lila home. She politely turned me down. She was going with Bausch, she said, because it was the middle of a Monday, and they needed to get back to work. That was the way of it with funerals. They came, they were done with, and for the rest of us, life went rolling right along.

We made dinner plans for the following Friday, but to hedge my bet, I told her I had something for her in the car. We walked over to my bucket, and I took the envelope from the glove box. She wrinkled her brow with curiosity as she slipped out the folded sheet of lined paper and opened it.

She ran a finger along the one ragged edge, and I could tell the words written on the page made no sense to her. But the numbers were a clue. She looked up from it with wide eyes. "My God, is this...?"

"Yeah," I said. I traced my finger under the handwritten lines. "Those are the names of two banks in Switzerland, and those are the account numbers."

"But I don't see…why give this to me?"

"Well, for one thing, you're the closest thing he had to an heir."

"Is that legal?"

I laughed. "Honey, we're talking about blackmail money. None of this is legal." I closed her hand around the paper. "That doesn't mean it's not right."

"Oh, but Nate, I can't." She shook the paper at me. "This is all such dirty money."

"You know," I said, "a very classy dame I know once pointed something out to me. No money's ever really clean." I laid my hands on hers. "But I'm guessing you'll find cleaner uses for it than any of the previous owners."

I didn't want to give her a chance to argue any further, so I gave her a quick kiss on the forehead and climbed into the car.

"See you Friday," I said and drove away.

I was disappointed, but not surprised, when Friday rolled around and Lila called to cancel on dinner, with a vague promise to maybe try again the following week. I was less surprised when I tried calling her that next week and her phone service had been disconnected. I tried her at the Global Travel Bureau, and Herm Bausch said she'd quit her job with some hazy talk about moving to San Francisco, or possibly Buffalo.

I wasn't happy about it, but I understood. After all she'd been through with Cecil Whitcanack and his bughouse daughter, plus whatever griefs she'd already been carrying around, I supposed L.A. had become the capitol city of bad memories for her. She needed a clean break and a fresh start. I had no idea how much money Whit had tucked away, but I suspected Lila would have enough to buy both those things anywhere she chose.

Chapter Twenty

For better or worse, Alan Whitcanack's subtle and non-descript funeral had suited the quiet sort of person he was. Charlie Dubek's funeral, held the following day, likewise suited its guest of honor. Just like the guy himself, it was big, loud, and brash. It brought L.A. corruption and hypocrisy out on pompous parade, dolled up for the festivities in a paper-thin layer of respectability. I skipped it but could hardly miss reading about it in the newspapers. It was page one with photos in all the local rags. You'd have thought Roosevelt himself had shuffled off this mortal coil.

Civic and government leaders and local nabobs turned out en masse to publicly show off their black armbands and solemn faces. Among the dignitaries, the papers tallied a former governor, a state senator, and three county supervisors. Rounding out the roster were my old pal, District Attorney Buron Fitts, my old boss Sheriff Eugene Biscailuz, and LA's new police chief, Arthur Hohmann. Mayor Fletcher Bowron, of course, was among the mourners, and he offered the newspapers and radio stations his personal eulogy for the deceased.

"It can be said without question," I read in a black-bordered section titled "The Mayor's Tribute" on the *Times* front page, "that the city of Los Angeles has lost a great supporter and a potent force for change and progress in our community. Through his generous contributions, his advocacy, and his advisership, Charles Dubek helped shape the policies that promoted prosperity and active growth both in our city and throughout the greater Los Angeles region. For myself, I have lost a trusted friend and ally."

A motorcycle escort of officers from the Highway Patrol and L.A.P.D.

led the way down York Boulevard from St. Ignatius of Loyola Church to Dubek's last stop, at a mausoleum in Forest Lawn Memorial Park. The *Times* piece included a quarter-page photo of the cortege stretching from the motor coppers out front for as far as the camera's eye could see. What the camera couldn't capture, and the papers didn't trouble to remark on, was the large number of private cars in the jalopy junket that were outfitted with bulletproof glass. I suspected that had the boys with badges who were forced to lead the procession been able to turn around and start emptying out all those shiny Packards and Caddies, the city would have ended up all but empty of crooks, and the state pens would have been stuffed like Thanksgiving turkeys.

If there was any kind of ritual observance of Alanna Whitcanack's passing, I never heard about it. My guess would be she was shipped off from Doc Reese's care to the county crematorium and ended up in a cheap urn buried in an unmarked patch of weeds in the county's boneyard. Maybe not a necessary end, but a fitting one.

The grim and gloomy business over and done with, happier times were ahead. Mikey left the hospital after a week and was on the mend. Since fingerprint work didn't require full use of both arms, I was able to throw a little work his way while he recuperated and convinced a couple of my competitors to do likewise. Since he was mostly housebound for the time being, he was able to put nearly all the money it earned him into his college kitty.

By mid-August, the sling was gone. A regular routine of exercises and hot water treatments were paying off, and Mikey's doctors said if he kept at it, he'd have the shoulder and arm in good working order by the end of the year.

But that wasn't the only cause for celebration. Mikey's birthday was the 21st of August, and he'd be leaving the week after that for college. I'd offered to contribute something to the college fund, but both Mikey and his old man scotched that idea. Mikey said he'd find a part-time job in Berkeley. He knew it wouldn't be easy, but he was determined to gut it out on his own.

So I was left doing the next best thing, which wasn't much, but it wasn't nothing. Dusty, Pooter, and I put together a party for the kid—a sort of combined getting-out-of-the-hospital, going-off-to-college, birthday party.

The boys agreed to close the Buscadero for our private shindig the Saturday before Mikey's birthday. Saturday being their busiest night, I thought that was contribution enough, but Pooter insisted on financing the whole thing. So Dusty and I were left to handle the organizing. We'd decided to make it a surprise.

We cooked up a tale that someone had busted into the Buscadero and done a punch job on the safe, and we needed Mikey to dust it inside and out. Pooter was distraught, we explained, because they had stolen his buckle from the 1921 Pendleton Roundup where he'd taken the top prize for calf roping.

Mikey bought the story, hook, line, and rodeo buckle. When the appointed night came, I picked him up at his place and withstood the usual ominous threats from his father, although there was a twinkle in Floyd's eye when he promised to visit bodily harm on me. We'd let him in on the gag, and he, of course, was more than happy to go along with any plan that ended in free booze. I had some pause in inviting him but decided he'd get drunk with us or without. At least this way, we could keep an eye on him.

I made an excuse to stop by the office to give Floyd time to get to the party. I called Pooter from there and told him we were on the way.

When I parked in front of the bar, Dusty met us on the sidewalk, looking properly aggrieved and explaining that Pooter was too upset even to leave the office. His day-playing in cheap Westerns was paying off—I almost believed him. I suggested that Mikey leave his print stuff in the car while we went in first to look things over.

We went inside the darkened saloon and were halfway to the bar when the lights kicked on, and everyone came out of hiding and yelled, "Surprise!" Mikey stood and stared for a moment, then looked a question at me. When he caught on, the look of joy on his face was worth all the irritation he'd ever given me.

The two old cowboys had gone all out decorating the place, and at that moment there wasn't a ballroom in L.A. that could have compared. The place was a carnival of colorful lights, balloons, streamers, and confetti. The rough tables were all covered with linen cloths. The boys had loaded up the

Symphonola with a few records more to Mikey's taste, so along with the usual cowboy fare, we had selections from Benny Goodman, Woody Herman, and Duke Ellington.

The turnout was good, considering the guest list had been left to Dusty and me, and the closest either of us had ever gotten to planning a party was beer and poker. Benjy came, along with his Uncle Gus and Aunt Sophia, who appeared to have called some sort of truce. Ray Pinker showed up, which was a help because he brought with him half a dozen of Mikey's classmates. One of the doctors who'd treated Mikey came, although Mikey seemed far happier that two of his nurses also turned up, along with a cute little blonde candy striper about Mikey's age. Floyd brought a couple of neighbors from their apartment building. Aggie Underwood even came along, but after I spotted her making notes more than once, I suspected her interest in the festivities was at least partly professional. And Monte was there, of course. He was the second most popular one in the room.

Mikey seemed to enjoy being the man of the hour, and I was proud of the kid that he took the honor seriously. He spent time talking with everyone there and made a point to thank each of them for coming.

Pooter had volunteered to handle food and promised a special dish. That dish turned out to be the one and only thing Pooter knew how to cook. It was an education to those of us reared in sunny Southern California to learn that there were distinct differences between what L.A. called "chili" and what Texans did. For one thing, Texans apparently didn't put beans in their chili. For another, they seemed to prefer it spiced and seasoned to the point that you'd need to stir in a spoonful or two of molten lava to cool it down. Not that it wasn't tasty—it was. But after the first sample, I was happy that we were in a bar and ice-cold beer was near at hand.

Soon everyone had tried the chili and turned to dousing their scorched throats with beer. In Mikey's and the other kids' cases, it was soda pop—at least while anybody was looking. About that time, two late arrivals walked in: Queenan and Lockwood. Monte spotted Queenan and began to growl. I quieted the big dog with a look.

They came straight over to the table where I sat, half listening to Benjy's

157

discourse on Mayor Bowron's clean-up campaign and what it meant for the city's future. I'd been sticking close to Benjy all evening in hopes I'd hear him introducing himself to a fellow partygoer. So far, nothing.

"I didn't think you boys would make it," I said.

"Well, Ross," Queenan replied with a serious face, "I wish I could say this was a social visit." He spoke in an overly loud voice, even though his usual speaking voice was nothing short of a foghorn. Out of the corner of his eye, he was watching Mikey, who sat at the next table talking to the candy striper girl. Mikey looked up at Queenan's words, then smiled and stood to greet the newcomers. Queenan fixed him with a hard stare and announced, "We got a call there's underage drinkin' goin' on in this joint."

Mikey and his smile froze in place. At the bar, a couple of the students suddenly remembered appointments they were late for and slunk out. As Queenan continued to eyeball Mikey, the kid found his voice and turned around to point to the glasses on his table.

"We're drinkin' ginger ale, Captain, honest. You can check it if you want."

Queenan leaned in until they were almost nose-to-nose. "Is that right, kid?" he said in a voice dripping with sarcasm. He leaned back again and, making a quick calculation, clapped Mikey on his good shoulder. "Well, what the hell for? It's your birthday, ain't it?" He cut loose with a bellowing laugh, and I couldn't tell whether the hard act or the laughter scared the kid more.

When he'd had a moment to recover, Mikey shook hands with the two cops and welcomed them. He gravely explained to Queenan that he didn't drink alcohol, anyway. That made me feel a little more secure about my office bottle.

Queenan pointed a thumb at me and said, "No shame in that, kid. Your boss here drinks enough for the both of you." The coppers both ordered drinks at the bar and came back to sit at my table. Queenan sat as far from Monte as he could.

Lockwood extended a hand to Benjy. "How you doing? Bill Lockwood."

"Ben Giannopoulos," Benjy said.

As Benjy and Queenan were making mutual introductions, I leaned over to Lockwood. "I owe you for that one, pal." He just gave me a curious look and saluted with his beer.

Aggie came over from the bar, sipping a sidecar. She swapped hellos with the two detectives and took the chair across from me. She flipped her notebook open to scribble something and, reading upside down, I saw she'd had written "High School Hawkshaw" at the top of the page. When she noticed me looking, she gave me an accusing look and slapped the notebook closed.

I leaned across the table. "He graduated high school last year, Ag," I told her. "He's off to Berkeley next week."

She made a face at me, opened the notebook again, and struck a line through her title. "Fine, killjoy. The hell with it—I'll think of something."

A few minutes later, the music stopped short as Dusty unplugged the Symphonola. Talk died down to a murmur while he went behind the bar to fiddle with a couple of switches. The lights dimmed, the swing door to the kitchen opened, and Pooter came out carrying a chocolate cake so big it took nearly his entire wingspan to manage it. His grinning face was haloed in the light of twenty candles.

He set the cake on Mikey's table, and we all gathered around. Pooter must have gone to one of the local deluxe bakeries; the cake was a pip. The top was covered with blue icing sculpted to look like ocean waves. There was a big white square on one side with a fingerprint drawn in black icing. On the other side, in brick-red icing, was what looked like the façade of a college building. Between them, in green icing, it said, "Happy Birthday, Michael," and under that, "Bon Voyage."

Mikey blew out the candles in one try, and everyone clapped and cheered. He looked around the room with a shy smile. "Thanks, guys."

After the cake, it was time for gifts. Mikey opened each one with a big smile and a word of thanks. Benjy gave him a nice fountain pen, and Ray Pinker gave him a fine set of camel hair fingerprint brushes. Dusty gave him a copy of Fricke's *Criminal Investigation*, newer than mine, and Pooter gave him a leather suitcase. His pop gave him a gray wool peacoat.

"Weather up north don't stay near as warm as it does down here," Floyd said with a catch in his voice.

Whether he intended it or not, Mikey opened my gift last of all. It was a brass nameplate, a duplicate of the one that sat on my desk. Engraved on it was "Michael 'Prints' Galvin."

"That's for when you come back here and take Pinker's job."

And nothing against Ray Pinker, but I half-hoped the kid would. I hoped he'd come back, anyway. I was going to miss having the little smart-ass around. Plus, he owed me some dog-sitting time.

I got a letter from Mike—funny how I could remember to call him that once he was gone—three weeks later. He'd gotten settled in, classes had started, and he'd made a new friend or two. The shoulder was coming along, and he was losing the numbness in his fingers. He had one big concern on his mind, and he asked me to swear on my word of honor that I hadn't secretly sent the college any money toward his schooling. It seemed he had arrived and gone more or less straight to the bursar's office to settle up for his first semester. The clerk there informed him that he didn't owe anything for that term, or for any of his other terms. An anonymous benefactor, she told him, had paid his full four years' tuition in advance.

I didn't have to think long to know who the guilty party was. Lila was already putting Whit's money to better uses. For all the ways Charlie Dubek had been a wrong guy, he was right about one thing. Gone didn't mean you didn't still have reach.

About the Author

Award-winning author J.R. Sanders is a native Midwesterner and longtime denizen of the L.A. suburbs.

His nonfiction articles appear in such periodicals as Law & Order and Wild West magazines. His books include *Some Gave All*, which gives true accounts of forgotten Old West lawmen killed in the line of duty.

J.R.'s first Nate Ross novel, *Stardust Trail* - a detective story set among the B-Western film productions of 1930s Hollywood - was a 2021 Spur Award Finalist (for Best Historical Novel), and Silver Falchion Award Finalist (for Best Investigator).

Bring the Night is the third novel in the Nate Ross series.

SOCIAL MEDIA HANDLES:
  Linktree: linktr.ee/jrsanders
  Facebook: facebook.com/authorjrs
  Instagram: Instagram.com/jrsanderswest
  YouTube: youtube.com/@JRSanders

AUTHOR WEBSITE:

www.jrsanders.com

Also by J. R. Sanders

Dead-Bang Fall (Level Best Books, 2022)

Stardust Trail (Level Best Books, 2020)

Some Gave All: Forgotten Old West Lawmen Who Died With Their Boots On (Moonlight Mesa Associates, 2013)